A COLLECTI... ...768

IT'S BEGINNING
TO LOOK A LOT LIKE
Christmas

CHRIS TURNBULL

Text Copyright © 2017 Chris Turnbull
Cover by Lorena Martin from www.premadeebookcovers.co.uk
Formatting by Jumping Jack Graphics

ISBN: 197926807X
ISBN-13: 978-1979268073

For Rhonda & Barbara

Our most bonkers, Christmas loving, friends

ALSO BY CHRIS TURNBULL

The Vintage Coat
Carousel
D: Darkest Beginnings
D: Whitby's Darkest Secret
D: Revenge Hits London

A Home For Emy – Children's Book

CONTENTS

CHRIS TURNBULL

It's
Beginning To
Look A Lot
Like
Christmas

How Do You Say, Merry Christmas?

Glaedelig Jul – Danish

Vrolijike Kerst – Dutch

Hyvvaa Joulua – Finnish

Joyeux Noël - French

Frohe Weihnachten – German

Kala Christouyenna – Greek

Gledileg Jol – Icelandic

Buon Natale – Italian

God Jul – Norwegian

Feliz Natal – Portuguese

Feliz Navidad - Spanish

Heri za Krismas – Swahili

God Jul – Swedish

Iyi Noeller – Turkish

And the ever popular "Merry Christmas"

Robin Redbreast

Kate sat staring out of her bedroom window. She could see her mother in the garden bringing in the washing. The garden was not overly large, but it did over look fields and woodlands in the distance; and the rolling hills beyond were a magical sight that changed with every season. It was the end of November, and a rare nice day in the English countryside.

As Kate watched her mother she saw next doors cat stroll into the garden. A fat tabby cat that was often found sunbathing on their lawn.

'Shoo.' She heard her mother shout at it, as it tried to steal her underwear from the laundry basket. Kate cried in hysterics of laughter as the cat made a dash for the fence, carrying one of her mother's socks. 'Pesky animal.' She hollered as the cat escaped into the field and ran out of sight.

Kate sat and watched out of her window often, she enjoyed seeing the birds that flew by, and often she would see rabbits in the field playing. She was about to move away from the window when something caught her eye. It was a robin. The small bird with glossy wings and bright red chest perched on her window ledge for a moment, it seemed to be trying to reach something. Kate stayed as still as she possibly could so as not to frighten the little bird, and watched as it tried to get a large feather that had attached itself to a brick. Finally with the feather in its mouth the robin flew away, soaring over her garden and landing in a small evergreen bush positioned at the opposite side of the fence. Kate watched as it jumped between the branches before disappearing inside.

Over the next few weeks Kate kept a look out for the little robin. It was often seen around the garden and occasionally visiting the bird feeder Kate's mum had proudly set up back in spring.

As December approached the bird feeder got less and less visitors as the native birds migrated, yet the little robin still made its daily visit.

'Kate shall we get the Christmas tree this afternoon?' Mum asked one Saturday afternoon.

'Yes, yes, yes!' Kate cheered, and quickly helped her mother fetch the decorations from the loft. 'Mummy…' Kate spoke in a serious voice after checking their Christmas boxes, '…we have nothing in here with a robin on?'

Mother glanced at the explosion of decorations that now littered the living room floor and smiled.

'Maybe a new piece is in order. Get your coat Kate, we will go get a tree and a new ornament.' Kate's mum grabs the keys and locked the door behind them, and they were soon in the car on their way. There was a garden centre only ten minutes' drive away and they had been advertising Christmas trees for the past few weeks. Kate was so excited that she raced into the shop and started looking for something with a robin on it. It did not take her long as robin statues, tree decorations and even lights were all in the shape of robins.

'Which one would you prefer darling?' Kate was so overwhelmed by the choice that she could not choose. They both spent the next ten minutes looking at all the festive adornments before Kate finally settled on a robin which had been painted on a small round piece of glass, and attached to the back was a small candle holder so as to light up the little bird.

'Great choice.' Kate's mum approved, 'now let us get a tree and we can go home and decorate it with some nice hot chocolate to reward our hard work.' Kate left choosing the tree down to her mother. They had a real tree every year, the fern smell that gave the house the most delightful aroma was a sign that Christmas was coming. Her mother loved to touch the branches and even smell the trees up close before purchasing one, just to make sure she was getting the most fragrant one possible.

Back home and the tree was placed into its metal stand and left in the centre of the room whist mother untangled the fairy lights. Once the lights were finally on Kate would decorate the tree with an almighty number of baubles, trinkets and scented cinnamon sticks.

With the tree finally finished and positioned perfectly in the window and the glass robin candle holder on display above the wood burner, they finally settled down with a mug of hot chocolate. The house was always warm and cosy at this time of year, and Kate loved seeing the wood burner in fully glow. They settled in for the evening with a Christmas movie, another tradition that they enjoyed.

Outside was now dark, and their cottage was on the edge of a village where the streetlamps did not reach. It was peaceful and picturesque. A storm was beginning to muster, and the sound of the wind howled as rain began to beat hard against the window.

When the film was finished Kate went to bed. Her view of the garden non-existent in the darkness, but the sound of the storm made clear what was happening. 'Take care little robin.' Kate whispered closing her curtains and returning to her bed.

Morning came quickly and the sun shone through the curtains as through last night's storm had never happened. However Kate almost screamed upon what she saw when she threw open the curtains. The garden chairs had been thrown into the field, the fence was no longer in view and the ever green bush that housed the little robin was now hidden from sight due to a large oak tree that had fallen during the storm.

Kate quickly tied her dressing gown and ran downstairs and into the kitchen where her mother stood. 'Are you okay Kate…' she had no time to reply to her mother, nor did she have time to put on her shoes. She ran barefoot across the damp grass and started to search between the branches of the fallen oak. She managed to find the ever green brush quite quickly, however there was no sign of the little bird.

'Kate, come back in here, you'll catch your death in this temperature.' Kate was about to give up when she heard a small chirping noise. Hidden beneath some leaves was the little robin, it tried to fly away from Kate but fell straight back down onto the ground, its right wind bent over on itself. 'Stay there.' Kate demanded of the robin, and she quickly ran back towards the house.

'Kate, darling whatever came over you?' Kate again ran straight past her mother and dashed upstairs to her bedroom once more. She opened up her cupboards and pulled out an old shoebox. Inside the box she had hundreds of shells and colourful rocks that she had collected on various visits to the seaside. In one swift movement she emptied the content of the box and ran back out into the garden with it.

The robin was exactly where she had left it, its chirping much louder now. 'Come now little robin, I won't hurt you.' Kate managed to encourage the little bird into the box, she closed the lid for safety and carried it back to the kitchen where her mother was still standing in the doorway.

'Now young lady,' her mother was furious, 'I want an explanation for this behaviour.' Kate didn't say a word and simply opened up the box for her mother to see the robin that was hiding in the corner. Kate's mum gasped upon seeing the injured animal. 'We need to take it to the vet and ask advice on what to do.' Kate didn't hesitate and dashes back upstairs to dress as quickly as she could.

The drive to the vets wasn't long, and they were seen almost immediately. Vet nurse Lesley was more than happy to examine the robin and reassured Kate that he was going to be okay.

Lesley used tape to bandage up the wing, and used it to hold the wing firmly against its own body. She then injected the bird with a mild pain relief before placing it back in the box. 'Now let us just watch him for a few minutes to make sure he can walk okay. I don't want to the tape to be too tight.' Kate watched anxiously as the little robin stood and examined the tape. He then stretched out his good wing and tried to jump out of the box. 'I think he will be more than fine. Are you happy for me to take him into the back where we can keep an eye on him for the next few days?'

'But he is my robin.' Kate mumbled, 'he lives in my garden, I want to take him home.' Lesley smiled and closed the shoe box lid. 'Allow me to give you some information on his diet before you leave then, he will need to be strong again before he can return to the garden.' Lesley handed Kate's mum some leaflets and they left for home.

Kate turned the shoe box into a nest for the tiny robin. She placed it on her window ledge so that he had a perfect view of the garden. She collected leaves and small twigs from the garden, and used a small hand towel to pad it out. She also used an egg cup as a drinking bowl and brought some of the bird feeder treats in from the garden too.

By the next morning Kate was worried about the little bird, its water bowl was untouched and the food which had been left was intact. 'Come on little one, you must eat and get stronger if you want to go back into the garden.' The robin stayed curled up in the nest fir the duration of the day, barely moving and looking extremely sorry for itself.

By nightfall the bird was still restless and had not yet eaten or drunk. Kate's mum saw the sadness in her daughters eyes and tried to think of something to cheer her up. 'Would you like to watch another Christmas film this evening?' Kate shrugged her shoulders, her eyes still fixed upon the helpless bird. Her mother then left her room in a rush and her footsteps could be heard hurrying down the stairs. The noise of the backdoor opening caused Kate to watch from her window, she was curious as to what her mother was up to. She saw her go into the garden shed, and after a few second she immerged again. Nothing seemed different to when she had first entered the shed. What was she doing?

Kate listened as her mother's footsteps climbed back up the stairs and re-entered her bedroom. She looked up at her mother with a questioning expression upon her face. Quick to see her daughter's expression she placed her hand in her pocked and brought out a clenched fist. 'Do you remember when you were poorly, and you didn't want to eat very much?' Kate nodded, but was unsure where her mother was going with this. 'Well after two days I finally got you to eat some biscuits. It wasn't what you should have been eating, but I was pleased to see you finally have something.'

'But mum, we cannot feed the robin biscuits.' Kate sniggered at the thought.

'No darling, but this boring seed is not very exciting for him either. Maybe this will encourage him to eat.' She uncurled her fist to reveal a handful of dried mealworms. Kate's face lit up with joy and watched as her mother scattered them on along the base of the shoebox, near the robin. The sound of the mealworms falling into the box attracted his attention immediately and he sat up straight to see what had joined him. Slowly he got to his feet and came to the first mealworm, he played with it in his beak for a moment before breaking it into smaller pieces to eat. Kate wanted to cheer with excitement, but stopped herself so as not to frighten him. Then watched as he ate a number of the mealworms before reaching the egg holder where he finally started drinking.

The days that followed saw the bird's appetite grow. He was eating and drinking more each day. Kate would always make sure he had fresh water and food and even gave him fresh bedding. She found herself singing to him one evening and the little bird even chirped along with her.

A week after the accident they were back at the vets. Lesley was thrilled to see that the robin had put on some weight and that the broken wing was healing nicely. She re-dressed the wing with some clean tape and sent them on their way.

The following week they returned again to get the wing cleaned, and were surprised to hear that the wing was healed and no longer required dressing. 'However this doesn't mean that he is able to go back into the garden just yet.' Lesley explained, 'He will need a couple of days to get his strength back, after all his wings haven't be used in over two weeks.'

Kate took the little bird back into her room, he no longer wore his bandages and began to flap his wings as soon as the shoe box lid was lifted. He rose only inches before falling back into his nest. 'Don't worry little robin, you will do it soon.' It was now a week until Christmas and snow had begun to fall outside. Kate kept the bird company as she watched the snow fall past her window.

By mid-week the robin was flying around her room, it clung to her curtains before taking off again and landing on her bed. When Kate's mother walked in, she had to duck to avoid the little bird flying into her. 'I see he is strong enough to fly now, shall we let him go?' Kate's smiles turned to sadness upon hearing this. 'Do we have to?' She pleaded with her mother, although she knew deep down that he had to go at some point. 'One more night.' Mother said, her voice serious yet a sadness in her eye was evident.

The next day the snow had stopped and the ground lay white and fluffy. Kate knew she had to say goodbye to the little robin. She opened her window as wide as it would possibly go and whispered. 'Go now,

you're all better.' The robin looked into the snow covered garden, a fresh breeze blew through the window and the robin was soon perching on the window ledge looking out. The fallen tree had been taken away and the evergreen, although damaged, was still suitable as a home.

The robin stretched out his wings and allowed the breeze to carry him along over the garden. Kate watched as he soared over the garden shed, past the evergreen and into the field where he continued to fly until he was no longer in sight. Kate shed a tear, her shoebox empty and her robin gone.

3 Days Later…

It was Christmas morning and Kate woke her mother up at first light. Before presents they lit the wood burner and made some toast for breakfast. It had again snowed and Kate couldn't wait to build a snowman later that afternoon. As they ate their toast in the kitchen they were disturbed by an unusual knocking sound. Kate and her mother both looked towards the kitchen window at the same time, and there standing on the ledge was the robin. Its bright red chest and round little body a delight to see. It turned and flew away, both Kate and her mum jumped to their feet and raced to the window in the hope to see it. The robin landed in the evergreen, and upon landing Kate was surprised to see that he was not alone. A second robin shared the branch with him and they both retreated into the nest together. 'Look mum, mister robin has a girlfriend.' Kate clapped and cheered.

Fun Christmas Fact

POSTMEN in Victorian England wore red, and were often referred to as Robins. This lead to Christmas cards showing Robins delivering letters, and has gone on to see Robins symbolized with Christmas.

THE CHRISTMAS MORNING POST

A Letter to Santa Claus

A Poem

Dear Santa, it's me here writing to say
That this year I've been good in every way.
Those rare little things, an occasional blip
Barely even my fault and a mere minor slip.

For the chewing gum stuck in my sister's hair
Was the outcome of just a childish dare.
How was I to know of the mess it would make?
And the bald spot she'd get be the size of a lake.

Then was the time that I lost our pet dog,
I took him to the park for a play and a jog.
But my friends were there too, I tied him to a bench
then returned home without him, my mother spoke
French.

There was also the time that I broke Grandpas
greenhouse
But the fault here lies more with a small field mouse.
For it ran down the garden and into the grass
And the ball I threw at it smashed straight through
the glass.

And who can forget when the fire engine came,
I was trying to cook when the pan grew a flame.
But my reason of course was it was Mother's day,
So surely this effort gives me a little leeway.

Then only last week was my other mistake,
During the school play I swore on the stage.
But again not my fault, I think you'll agree
For the manger collapsed and dug into my knee.

So with all this in mind, I think you can see
That these minor infringements can't be all blamed
on me.
I tried to be good and I mean that whole-hearted,
And I wanted you to know this before you departed.

So I plead not to be on the naughty list this year,
A present from you would make me give a cheer.
I hope I've convinced you that everything's fine,
So a very Merry Christmas, from Jack aged nine.

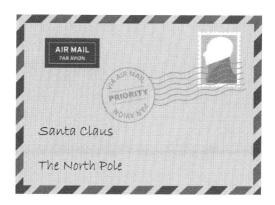

Fun Christmas Facts

THE first commercial Christmas cards were commissioned by civil servant Sir Henry Cole in London in 1843.

LONDON sweet maker Tom Smith created the first Christmas crackers in 1847, based on the sweet wrapper design.

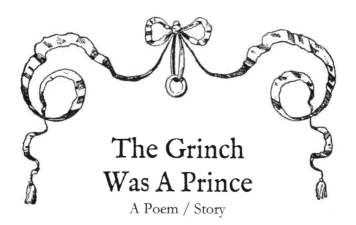

The Grinch
Was A Prince
A Poem / Story

You've heard of the Grinch, the one that stole
Christmas,
a nasty green creature with a plan most ambitious.
But the tale you were told was not the whole truth
So let us go back and re-tell from his youth.

The Grinch was a Prince, handsome, well bred,
born to be king once his father was dead.
But the prince he was spoiled, and grew up to be
selfish,
for he would turn up his nose, and leave peoples
dreams melted.

It was one Christmas Eve when things took a turn,
in his anger he threw things with the smallest
concern.
All the valuable china and antiques were smashed
but the Christmas tree took the brunt of the bash.

His father was furious and threw him straight out,
'Behavior like that won't get you the crown'.
In his anger he screamed 'Who needs you anyway'
then he stormed out of the castle in a violent rage.

The prince he took off through the snow covered
forest
he would never go back, and that was a promise.
Onward he travelled with no place to go,
his body turning blue and his face full of woe.

As darkness set in he began to lose hope,
in this worsening weather how was he to cope?
He had no water, no food and was miles from home,
and so perched under a tree he let out a groan.

Not too long passed when a light caught his eye,
twas a lantern torch from a mere passer-by.
the cloaked figure walked fast and took off through
the trees,
so the Prince began running and caught up in a
breeze.

'Pardon me' said the Prince in a tone of such pity,
'Please help direct me right back to the city.'
When the cloaked figure turned, the Prince couldn't
help stare,
for the maiden was pretty with the longest blonde
hair.

The maiden she smiled and offered him aid,
she lived just over the hill in house that she'd made.
A cottage as such, made of wood and old leaves,
a fragile little place that would be easy for thieves.

She lit them a fire and warmed up some food,
a large helping of mealworms chopped up and
stewed.
'What is this filth' he began to enrage
'Are you trying to kill me, you belong in a cage'

The maiden she cackled and threw the Prince out,
'Good luck in the forest' she said in a shout.
And as the door slammed and he stood back in the
snow,
the house disappeared in an impressive light show.

'A witch' thought the Prince, as he marched swiftly
away,
the sun was now rising, for it was Christmas day.
He walked and he walked till his feet became sore,
he walked till he just couldn't walk anymore.

The Prince surely knew he was running out of
choices,
then through the trees he began to hear voices.
He followed the sound and got such a delight,
for it was a town; he would be alright.

The town was called Whoville, what a funny old
name,
clearly whoever named it was a master of game.
The square was so busy with Christmas delight,
and when the Prince entered they all screamed with
fright.

Why were they screaming and acting so scared?
then the Prince caught his reflection and started to
stare.
His beautiful face was all green and all hairy,
his hand were like claws, all horrid and scary.

The Who's they stood strong and threw the Prince
out,
a monster like this would be trouble no doubt.
So the Prince left the town for the great mountain
tops,
Where he found a dry cave and decided to stop.

'How could this have happened' the Prince started to
cry,
'I'll bet it's the witch, and for this she will die.'
So the Prince began searching, he travelled each day,
but the witch was not found, so a monster he'd stay.

He returned to the castle, to his father he'd beg,
but recognised he was not, and threw out by his leg.
So he returned to the cave where he slept on the
floor,
and lived off the landfill that littered next door.

The months they passed by and the Prince he grew
bitter,
his power was little more than an oversized critter.
The town people never once gave him an inch,
and horribly named him the smelly old Grinch.

A year soon passed by and twas Christmas once
more,
and the Grinch was now bitter and twisted and sore.
'What was the big deal?' he thought with a huff,
'Come January first I'll end up with their stuff.'

The Grinch watched the Who's as they laughed and
they played,
the whole town was there, even the fire brigade.
Then he thought to himself 'These people are poor'
he couldn't help wonder 'what they're so happy for?'

A few years passed and the Grinch had a plan,
this Christmas fiasco, he wasn't a fan.
The Who's with their happy festive abode,
would be punished for the hatred to the Prince that
they showed.

The next part of the story is the bit that you know,
he stole the Who's Christmas in the thickest of snow.
But as we all know it was saved again too,
by a young little girl called Cindy Lou Who.

So the Prince never got to be king of the land,
and remained with his green hairy monstrous hands.
But thanks to Cindy Lou he was welcomed to dinner,
and for the first time in years he felt like a winner.

Fun Christmas Fact

IN 1647, the English parliament passed a law which made Christmas illegal. The Puritan leader Oliver Cromwell, who considered feasting and revelry on what was supposed to be a holy day to be immoral, banned the Christmas festivities. The ban was lifted only when Cromwell lost power in 1660.

Princess Nathalya

Friday 12th December 1941

The steam engine came to a stop with an almighty screech of the brakes. It was dark out, and the small station platform was barely visible was it not for a single lamp against the wall. It was the last stop of the night, and the carriages emptied as the passengers piled out into the bitter cold. All of them mere children and not one of them spoke. Thirty of them in total, all stood and waited for what felt like hours in the winter breeze. Eventually a small bus pulled up and a woman in her late fifties emerged.

'Oh good heavens, the train wasn't expected

for another ten minutes. I am so sorry children for leaving you in the cold. Quickly get aboard we will do a name check once inside.' She seemed a pleasant enough woman, her bobbed hair was silver and she dressed like an old fashioned school teacher. 'My name is Mrs Rosser and I will be the one looking after you during your stay. Come along now, let's get on board quickly.' Still none of the children spoke as they filed onto the bus. They had been travelling for most of the day and their exhaustion was clear.

The last child to get onto the bus was also the smallest. Heather Leanne was just seven years old, she had beautiful long blonde curly hair and carried her favourite teddy bear with her. Some of the older children called her Goldilocks, but they did not say it in a complimentary tone.

Heather sat by herself on the bus, looking out of the window. It was so dark outside that she could barely even make out the road. It was only a short drive to where they were staying, and Heather was surprised when they arrived outside what looked like a castle.

'Welcome children to Armathwaite Hall.' Mrs

Rosser said as they made their way off of the bus. 'Now let us get inside where it is warm, and I can direct you all to your dorms.' The huddle of children followed quickly. The dark night was bitterly cold and the ground was beginning to sparkle in the moon light as frost began to set.

The manor house was indeed an impressive sight from the outside, even in the dark, but once through the large oak doors the interior was even more remarkable. A large stone staircase dominated the entrance hall, with an enormous chandelier hanging above it. There was a roaring fire to the side of the hall, which the group of children immediately hovered around. Mrs Rosser spilt the children into boys and girls, telling the boys to stay by the fire she asked all the girls to step forward.

'Now young ladies I have three rooms for you, so let me check my list of names against you all.' She called out each girl in turn, and each time a quiet reply of 'Here' was heard from the group. When she got to the end of the list Heathers name had not been read out.

'Excuse me Miss.' She said, tugging at Mrs Rosser's dress. 'You did not say my name.' Mrs Rosser smiled back at Heather and asked for her name.

'I don't seem to have you written down my dear. Are you sure you were supposed to come to Armathwaite?' Heather held out the paper label that was looped around her neck, all the evacuees had these. On the front was written her name, and on the back it said 'Armathwaite Hall. Final Stop.'

'Well then,' Mrs Rosser replied, 'I guess you are right. Not to worry, we will find you somewhere. Follow me girls.' They followed her up the carpeted staircase and along the corridor which was filled with portraits of elegant looking men and women. Mrs Rosser stopped at the first door and invited handfuls of girls inside. The rooms had been made up with five beds in each, but there was sixteen girls including Heather. At the last room Mrs Rosser told Heather to stay and wait, and within minutes she returned with bedding and a pillow.

'I'm afraid I don't have another bed for you to use, however I have a selection of pillows we can made into a comfortable area for you on the floor.' Heather was exhausted and helped Mrs Rosser set up the blankets and pillows under the window. None of the other girls in the room helped and got themselves ready for bed in silence.

'Good night everybody, sleep well. I will return in the morning to show you where breakfast will be served.' Mrs Rosser left and the room of silent girls began to finally speak. The girls in Heathers room were all around twelve years old, they had spoken briefly on the train and were already beginning to form friendships, however Heather had nobody her own age and was left out. The girls all piled onto one bed as they talked about the journey, the manor house and the boys. Heather walked over in the hope to be invited into the conversation, but she was told to go away by them all.

Heather returned to her bed, which looked more like a dog bed than something for humans. Still she did not blame Mrs Rosser who seemed to be a very nice woman.

In the morning Mrs Rosser burst in and was full of life.

'Morning girls, get dressed, I will be back in ten minutes to take you down for breakfast.' It didn't take them that long as they all only had the clothes they arrived in and a night dress. When Mrs Rosser returned they were all waiting at the door for her. They were taken down into a large dining room that had been set up with two large tables, one for the girls and one for the boys. There wasn't quite as many boys as there was girls. An older woman who was not introduced to them came around with bowls of porridge. It was the best thing Heather had tasted in a long time. The large windows of the room looked down towards a huge lake, Heather had heard about the Lake District being beautiful but she had not expected it to be this lovely. She couldn't take her eyes from the beautiful view all through breakfast.

Mrs Rosser spent the rest of the morning showing the children around the house and gardens. The outside of the building was even more impressive now in the daylight. She also walked them down towards the lake.

'If you are still here in the summer this is a beautiful place to swim.' She told them. Most of the children was getting cold and had no interest in being outside. Mrs Rosser realised this and took them back to the hall for lunch. After lunch Heather took herself off into the garden to explore some more. She loved the outdoors and even in the winter was more than happy to wrap up warm and spend as much time as she could playing out. She found a swing hanging from a tree and played on it for a little while. It looked back towards the house where she could see the window she slept beside. The girls she shared with were back in the room looking out at her as though she was something unnatural; they couldn't understand why anybody would happily be out in the cold when the manor was so toasty warm. She continued to explore the gardens which seemed to go on for miles. Different areas had different themes.

There was a vegetable garden, that currently lay bare other than a frosted over green house. There was a garden area that was mostly paved over with seating and a water feature in its centre. Finally she came to a garden that she liked the best, it was a walled garden that could be entered by a simple stone archway. Inside everything was currently dead, but the sheer

amount of trees and bushes made her excited for spring; it was clearly a colourful garden. A small lawned area in the middle had a stone bench on it, and Heather sat here for a short time taking in the garden. A robin was exploring the garden too, and she watched it as it made its way around looking for food.

The afternoon was getting on and darkness was starting to fall over the garden. Heather made her way back to the grand house and was pleased to be back in the warmth. She sat by the fire in the entrance hall for a while before returning to her dorm. Inside the dorm the other girls immediately stopped talking as she entered the room. Heather knew they didn't like her and she walked passed them and returned to her own bed. Mrs Rosser had gotten them all some new, second hand, clothes and the ones for Heather had been left on her bed. As she began to change into them she noticed that her teddy bear was no longer next to her pillow as she had left it. She began to move the blankets and pillows in a panicky pursuit; upon seeing her searching the other girls began to giggle.

'What have you done with it?' Heather screamed, trying not to cry. None of the girls spoke, but they continued to smirk and giggle. In the corner of her eye Heather noticed a piece of bedding trapped in the window. As she approached it she could see that her teddy bear had been tied to the sheet and was dangling from the window. Without thinking she opened the window and the sheet slid out causing her teddy bear to fall to the ground below. Now crying

Heather raced from the room and at full speed ran down the staircase and into the back garden where she found him lying unhurt.

The days and weeks that followed saw Heather more and more isolated from the group. They refused to speak to her and would often hide her belongings or mess up her bed so she had to remake it. Mrs Rosser was unaware of the issues, but was always pleasant to Heather when they spoke. Heather spent the majority of her time in the garden, her time spent between the jetty by the lake where she watched wildlife, and the walled garden. Mrs Rosser was aware of her outdoor activates and once joined her on a walk around the gardens to tell her about all the flowers that would be coming back in spring. Heather loved this, and was able to imagine all the beautiful flowers and butterflies that brightened up the currently drab looking land.

On Christmas Eve Mrs Rosser took the children to church. It was a tiny village church that was filled with hundreds of candles. Heather had been taken to church many times by her parents, and even more so with her mother after her father went off to war.

Christmas morning at Armathwaite Hall was no different to any other day for the evacuees. Mrs Rosser called them all for breakfast as usual and as expected there was nothing special other than her wishing everybody a 'Merry Christmas.' The dining room was normally full of life in a morning, but today everybody's spirits were a little down, it was the children's first Christmas without their families.

Once she had finished eating Heather took off into the garden as normal. It was a cloudy day and the overnight frost was still sparkling throughout the garden. Today she walked straight past the main gardens and decided to first go to the walled garden, it was by far he favorite of them all. She had hoped for snow so as to build a snowman, but so far none had arrived. When she arrived at the walled garden she almost gasped in disbelief at what she saw. The stone archway leading into the garden was now covered in a large wooden door. She approached the door cautiously, had Mrs Rosser put this here to stop her going in? Heather turned the door knob but the door was locked. In the corner of her eye she could see something peeking out from behind the ivy that climbed up the wall, it was a large rusty set of keys. She unhooked them, they were heavier than she had anticipated, and tried each of the keys one by one until she found the one that unlocked the door. Heather gave the thick door an almighty push, and was surprised that it released with ease. She pushed open the door and peaked around it to see it anybody was inside. Heather stared at what she saw before her, the garden was no longer dead and wintered. Now the daffodils were in flower around the grass lawn, the brightest pink and white blossom filled the trees and the flowers and bushes were all starting to green again ready to flower; it's as though Spring had arrived to the garden already. Heather stood in the doorway in surprise. She looked back over her shoulder to see the grey dead of winter that loomed over the other gardens, so why was the walled garden already flowering?

She pushed the door wider and entered, closing it again behind her. There was nobody else here. A swing had appeared from one of the trees, and Heather immediately sat upon it and looked out onto the beautiful garden.

'What are you doing?' A voice from behind her said. A young girl about Heathers age appeared; she had long dark curly hair and large brown eyes. She had a tanned complexion and wore a beautiful long pink dress. Heather jumped off of the swing in surprise.

'Hi, my name is Heather. Who are you?'

'I am Princess Nathalya, but you can call me Thalya for short. What are you doing in my garden?'

'Your garden? I didn't know you lived here too. I have been visiting the garden every day, I haven't seen you before.'

'This garden was made for me before I was born. Look, can you see the holly bush in the corner, that was planted the day I was born.' Heather could see it, it was one of the only plants in the garden that had any colour to it when she first visited.

'Do you know why the garden is starting to bloom already?' Heather asked.

'Already?' Thalya seemed confused by the question. 'I'm sure I don't know what you mean.' Heather was confused, but decided not to question her any more.

'Okay well I am sorry to be in your garden. I will leave.' She began heading back towards the door.

'No wait. Do you not want to stay and play?' Heather was delighted by the invitation; she had not played with any other child for a long time. Thalya jumped onto the swing and demanded to be pushed; Heather went along with it for a short while before asking to have a go. Soon the girls were laughing and playing as though they were old friends. Heather had not felt this good in months.

Soon the blossom on the trees began to fall around them like snow, the girls laughed and danced though it. When it eventually stopped Heather realised that the blossom had already been replaced with leaves, and even the daffodils had died back and been replaced by an array of beautiful flowers. The garden no longer looked as though spring had arrived, but rather that summer was in full bloom. The garden was filled with the sweetest smelling lavender, rose bushes of many colours, poppies and a whole array of colourful flowers that she had never seen before. The garden was also filled with butterflies, bumblebees and birds which could be heard singing in the trees above them.

'Thalya is this a magic garden?' asked Heather. She felt silly for asking, but what other reason could there be?

'Why do you ask?' Thalya replied. By the look on her face she couldn't understand what Heather was meaning. This made Heather even more curious, she began to wonder who Thalya was. Was she really a Princess, or was she some kind of magical being?

'I have some skipping ropes in the corner. Want to play?' Thalya changed the subject.

'Yes please.' The girls laughed and played the

entire day, Thalya was clearly enjoying having company in her garden, and Heather was thrilled to have finally made a friend. Thalya had a selection of games for them to play, and the afternoon soon passed by in the blink of an eye.

Without realising the garden was again changing, this time the leaves were putting on a beautiful display of oranges, yellows and browns. The girls hadn't noticed that the flowers were also dying back until the leaves of the trees began to fall at their feet.

'Winter arrives faster every year doesn't it.' Thalya said. Heather was a little taken by this comment, surely a seven year old girl hasn't experienced that many Winters. Heather simply agreed with her so as not to cause offence. The garden was starting to get darker as the sun set, and Heather knew that she would need to leave soon. Thalya didn't want her to go and begged her to stay a little longer.

'I'm sorry but if I return after dark fall I will be in trouble.' Said Heather, saddened to have to leave. 'We can play again tomorrow if you'd like?'

'Okay then.' Thalya replied. 'But I get first go on the swing.'

'Agreed.' Heather laughed. She returned to the door, taking one last look at the garden that was now almost bare again. Thalya gave her a little wave before Heather left. 'Are you not coming too?' She asked Thalya, 'It will be dark soon.'

'I think I will stay a little longer.'

Heather ran back to the house as quickly as she could, it was after nightfall and she knew she would be in trouble if caught by Mrs Rosser. Many of the children were still downstairs, and Heather managed to sneak into the sitting room undetected where she stayed to warm herself up before returning to her room for the night.

The next day Heather couldn't wait for breakfast to be over. She ate as quickly as she could and as soon as the room was dismissed she leaped out into the garden and ran as fast as she could towards the walled garden. When she arrived the doorway was gone, and the stone arch was empty like before. Confussed, Heather made her way into the wintery garden.

'Thalya?' she shouted, but no reply came. The swing was also gone. She sat on the stone bench and looked around; despite everything being dead she could picture the flowers in every boarder, bush and tree.

'Heather?' came a voice from the archway. Heather sat up in expectation, but it was not who she expected. Mrs Rosser walked into the garden. She was wrapped up warm. 'Here you are child. Are you alright?'

'I was looking for Thalya, do you know if she is coming to play today?' Mrs Rosser's eyes widened.

'Thalya? When did you meet somebody with that name?' she asked, sitting on the bench next to Heather.

'Yesterday Miss. We played in the garden all day together.' Mrs Rosser looked around the garden, her face saddened.

'Come inside Heather, I have managed to get you a bed. It was just delivered. I'm afraid it won't fit in the room with the other girls, but I think I will put you in Nathalya's old room. It hasn't been used in nearly sixty years that room, I think you will like it though as it has one of the best views of the gardens.' Mrs Rosser took Heather by the hand and led her back into the house. She took her to the top floor and into a bedroom that had no furniture in. She was right about the view, it looked over the gardens and even the lake was just about visible.

'Miss, who is Thalya?' Heather asked whilst admiring the view.

'She was a beautiful young girl, who once lived in this house. She was born on Christmas eve long before you or I was born.'

'Oh, I see.' Heather backed away from the window, but to the surprise of Mrs Rosser she did not seem sad. 'At least I had a friend on Christmas.'

Fun Christmas Facts

THE first Christmas celebrated in Britain is thought to have been in York in 521AD.

I Wish It Could Be Christmas

A Poem

I wish it could be Christmas
every day you say
The lights and decorations
Make the house so bright and gay

Of course you would want Christmas
to be every single day
For you don't have screaming children
and you don't have bills to pay

It's me who has to cook the dinner
And entertain the guests
The turkey is always overdone
And everyone wants the breasts.

I alone must wrap the gifts
And buy most of them too
All I crave is a short break
To sit down with a brew.

A taxi driver I often feel
Taking you to all your parties
With little time to catch a snack
I run on tea and smarties

The family are all together
With arguments a plenty
But not for anything that bad
Just because their glass is empty

Now don't think I hate Christmas
I love it in every way
But for goodness sake forgive me
If I don't want it every day

Fun Christmas Facts

EBENEZER Scrooge's famous line "Bah Humbug" almost never existed. Charles Dickens' initial choice was "Bah Christmas."

Christmas Spirit
A Modern Day Scrooge Story

The sound of the telephone rang throughout the house. It was the third time in less than ten minutes that it had rung; clearly somebody wanted to be spoken to.

Finally the home owner picked up the receiver. He was an old man and had been sat next to it the whole time.

'Yes.' His voice was hoarse and stern.

'Oh thank goodness,' came the voice of a younger woman, 'I've been trying to reach you for the past two days. Is everything okay?'

'Grand.'

'I'm just checking if you are coming for Christmas dinner tomorrow, Dad?' There was a moments pause, and for a second she thought the phone had cut out.

'Hello?'

'I'm still here.'

'We can pick you up if you like, saves you driving, you can have a drink then. Jacob and Zack are looking forward to seeing their Grandad.'

'I think I will pass this time love. I'm not a big eater and I don't want to spoil the festivities for the boys.'

'Don't be silly Dad, we all want you to be here. Surely it'll be better than being alone tomorrow? We should all be together on Christmas day, this year more than ever.' There was yet another pause.

'No love, I just want to be alone. Enjoy your day and I will phone the boys tomorrow evening.' And with that he hung up. Sat upon the wooden sideboard, next to the telephone was an old dusty frame. The man ran his finger across the pane of glass to better reveal the picture hidden beneath all the dust. It was a black and white photograph of his wedding day, some sixty years ago. A tear weld in the corner of his eye, and he lifted his glasses to wipe it away quickly. This would be his first Christmas without his beloved Marie, taken from him back in the summer after a short battle with cancer. The old man, named Fred, slouched back into his arm chair with a sigh. He was frail and walked much slower these past few months, but mostly he would stay in his chair. It was positioned close to the fire, and allowed him a perfect view out of the bay windows, as well as the television. His view was of the small front garden, where a bird feeder attracted all kinds of wildlife to it throughout the summer; but with winter firmly set he only now saw the little robin red breast.

The street was always quiet. Yet it was deserted of people and traffic due to the bitter cold. Fred turned on a couple of extra bars on his gas fire, and his living room was as warm as the Bahamas in no time. The glow of the fire lit up the room as the late afternoon brought with it darkness. Fred continued to sit in his chair and watch the world go by from his window. The little robin had been three times today.

By the time the street lamps came on, the threatening grey clouds finally burst and snow began to fall. Large flakes floated past the window and landed softly on the grass below.

Fred lit a small lamp positioned on a tall stand in the corner of the room, and a book resting nearby soon took his attention away from the falling snow outside.

There was a loud knock on his front door that woke him from a sleep, he then realised he had dozed

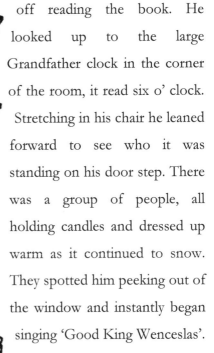

off reading the book. He looked up to the large Grandfather clock in the corner of the room, it read six o' clock. Stretching in his chair he leaned forward to see who it was standing on his door step. There was a group of people, all holding candles and dressed up warm as it continued to snow. They spotted him peeking out of the window and instantly began singing 'Good King Wenceslas'.

'Huh…' He grunted, and got out of his chair. The

choir outside now in full chorus. He opened his window to them and shouted, 'Clear off, or I'll phone the police and tell them you are harassing me.' With that the choir stopped, a gasp of shock at the old man's poisonous tone. Fred then slammed the window shut and drew the curtains.

'Good King Wenceslas indeed…' he mumbled to himself as he went through into the kitchen. 'The nerve of some people begging for money, and with a useless song like that. What's so bloody good about King Wenceslas anyway?' He made himself a sandwich, blue cheese, his favourite. Returning to his arm chair he switched on the television.

'Repeat, reality nonsense, repeat…' he muttered to himself as he flicked through the channels. 'Oh look, Home Alone. My Marie's favourite. What a load of rubbish, parents should be locked up for that kind of neglect.' He switched off the TV and dropped the remote onto a small table next to him, and returned to his book.

Before long he was asleep once more. The sound of the Grandfather clock ticking and his own gentle snores the only sounds to be heard through the house. Suddenly the man was awoken by the sound of the living room door slamming shut. 'What on earth.' He scolded, his heart beating fast and his eyes bolting wide open. Scanning around the room everything seemed to be normal, but as he was about to go back to sleep something caught his eye. The television was on. But hadn't he turned that off already? Despite the screen being on it was in complete silence, and the picture looked to be frozen. On the screen was a woman, she was beautiful with pale white skin and red fiery hair. She wore what could only be described as rags. She sat perfectly still against a blacked out background, and Fred could not take his eyes off of her.

After a moment of staring he reached down for the remote. 'Clearly frozen, stupid contraption.' He mumbled. But as he lifted the remote the woman turned her head and looked directly at Fred. He again froze in his chair and stared at the woman staring back at him with disbelief, what is this show? He wondered.

Fred clicked the off button on his remote, but instead of the television returning to its darkened blank screen, it lit up bright in a white light that filled the whole room. The woman, once sat within now standing beside it.

'Who are you?' Demanded Fred, a fear in his voice. 'Leave me alone.' The woman did not speak and the bright light of the television began to fade. 'I said who are you?' Fred repeated, his tone more stern this time. The woman dressed in rags smiled warmly at him and held out her hand to introduce herself. Fred hesitated at the gesture.

'My name is Noella, and I am the bringer of Christmas Spirit.' Her voice was soft, calm and sounded as though it echoed slightly.

'I beg your pardon?'

'This year you have lost your cheer, you have lost the true spirit of Christmas and I am here to show you that it is not too late to change your mind. Your daughter has invited you to dinner tomorrow, why have you declined this invitation?'

'Well...I...' Fred murmured in shock, how did this strange woman know this? 'Do you know my daughter? Did she send you here, because I do not want to spoil her and the children's Christmas with my miserable face. I am not exactly in the mood to be merry.'

'You have a beautiful daughter, but no we have not met. I am here because I know how much you will be missing if you do not go tomorrow.'

'You cannot convince me, and I would like you to leave my house now!' He was beginning to get angry. Yet despite this Noella's smiling expression never once faltered.

'There is something I wish to show you.' Said Noella, ignoring his demands for her to leave, and before he could reply she turned and placed one hand on the curtains, now closed over the bay window. In a blink of an eye the curtains vanished, and the window behind no longer looked the same, for in its place stood a giant sheet of glass reaching from floor to ceiling. Yet the view out onto the street still remained the same.

'What is all this!' Fred demanded, rubbing his eyes in disbelief. 'I am dreaming, this is all a dream. That's it. There is no other explanation. You're a figment of my imagination. I suspected that cheese was past its best, I was a fool to eat it.' Noella continued to listen as Fred tried to convince himself.

'Are you ready?' She asked.

'For what?'

'To be given back your Christmas Spirit?' Fred grunted and rolled his eyes at this.

'Nothing you can say will convince me, but since you are unwilling to leave I will humour you.' With that the pane of glass turned black, and the street view vanished from sight. Fred's armchair moved closer and when it stopped he was gobsmacked with what appeared before him. The large glass wall turned into a cinema like screen and before him he saw his daughter's living room. The Christmas tree in the corner was lit and presents filled the floor around it. Just then the door opened and in came Jacob and Zack, his grandchildren. They charged straight for the presents and were full of joy and delight. Behind them came their mother carrying a cup of coffee; but it was the next person to enter that made Fred gasp. It was Marie, his wife, followed closely by himself.

'Noella, what is this?' His brow was raised as he tried to understand what he was seeing.

'This is a picture of what happened last Christmas. Look how happy you all are.' He looked into the scene with a light in his eye and a smile on his face. The children were so giddy opening their gifts, and even more so helping to pass presents to their mother and grandparents. Watching his late wife opening a gift on the opposite side of the glass brought a tear to Fred's eye.

'She was sick even then, but you wouldn't know it to look at her. I think she knew in her heart that this could be her last Christmas.' Noella held out her hand, a tissue balanced between her fingers. 'Thank you.' He said, taking the tissue and wiping away the tears before they could fall.

'See the happiness in her eyes,' Noella spoke, 'even knowing what lie ahead she was determined to have a worthy family Christmas.'

'I know what you're trying to get at Noella, but last year she was here, last year we were all together. This year her presence will be missed so much that I fear the day will not be merry at all.' Noella turned back to face the glass screen, the scene of which had changed. Still showing scenes from last year the family were now around the dinner table eating their turkey. Fred carved the bird and handed out portions to everybody around the table, whilst Jacob and Zack pulled crackers with Marie and their mother, then taking it in turn to read the cheesy joke inside.

'Why was the turkey in the pop group?' Asked Zack,

'Because he was the only one with drumsticks!' The entire table burst into laughter. Even Fred sitting in his arm chair gave out a small chuckle.

'Your wife will be missed, for that I am certain, but everybody knows she would be there is she could.

If you do not go then the day will be dire, for you are more than able… so why would you not be there?' Noella's words hit Fred hard; he did not say another word as the scene before him disappeared once more.

The screen burst into colour again, and before him again was his daughters living room, they were all there opening their gifts. Confused he looked at Noella with a questioning look upon his face.

'I see you do not understand why I am showing you a similar scene.' He nodded and looked back, trying to figure out what was so different this time around. It was definitely a different Christmas to the one he had just watched, but surely nothing out of the ordinary.

'Look how happy everybody looks,' Noella gestured, 'can you tell me how long ago this was?' Fred frowned, he looked at Jacob and Zack who were noticeably younger.

'Three years ago maybe?' He couldn't really tell.

'Close. This was four years ago, the children are eight years old. Can you remember why this Christmas was unique and why I am showing it to you again?' Fred watched as his grandchildren opened their gifts, their smiles lighting up the entire room. Yet he could not think why this particular Christmas was so important.

'This is the Christmas,' Noella explained, 'that your daughter had to spend it without her fiancée, and her two children had to spend it without their father.' Fred's eyes widened.

'He left them.' He told Noella, 'Just like that, one day he packed his bags and left. They were all heartbroken.' He had to use the tissue again to catch his tears.

'Look into the faces of Jacob and Zack, look at your daughter laughing as they fool around by the tree. Those are the faces of brave people who are saddened by the empty space this Christmas, but they continue to support each other by putting on a cheerful face for one and other, and let the festive celebrations carry on. This does not mean they do not care, nor does it mean they have forgotten.'

'I understand what you are trying to teach me. I agree my family are strong and will cope, but what if I cannot? What happens then, answer me that!' The scene again went dark and the giant pane of glass returned to the view of the street outside.

'You do not know that,' Noella replied, 'but you must ask yourself this. Nobody knows what lies ahead, the next twelve months are as yet unwritten. But can you be certain that missing this Christmas day with your family is really what you want? To be alone at Christmas is not a sanctuary, but to some it is a cruel reality. You never know when your last Christmas will be, so it's important to keep Christmas well, and uphold the Christmas Spirit always.' Fred lowered his head, he knew what she was saying was true.

'Noella…' He looked up and she was gone. The window and curtains back to the way they had always been, the television turned off and the sound of the Grandfather clock ticking behind him. It was just after midnight, Christmas was here once more.

The next morning Fred rose early. Still convinced that Noella was nothing more than a strange dream conjured up by his out of date cheese, yet knowing that her message ort not to be ignored.

He washed and dressed as quickly as he could and headed out the door. His daughter only lived a short drive away. Upon pulling up outside he could see through the window that they had yet to open their gifts, the boys sat by the tree waiting for their mother to come through from the kitchen. He tapped on the window to get their attention.

'Grandpa's here!' They shouted hysterically, and ran from the living room to greet him at the front door.

'Merry Christmas Jacob, Merry Christmas Zack.' He said with a smile.

'Come on through Grandpa,' said Jacob, 'we are just about to open out gifts.' As he stepped through the door way their mother came through from the kitchen, investigating what all the commotion was about.

'Dad,' she embraced him tightly, 'thank you for coming.'

'Well it wouldn't be Christmas without us all being together now would it.' He said, closing the door behind him.

'What changed your mind?' She asked.

'Let's just say that the Spirit of Christmas gave me a good talking to.' He chuckled as they sat in the living room ready to distribute gifts.

Later that afternoon dinner was served, and as always the turkey was carved by Fred. He had Marie in his mind throughout the whole day, yet instead of sadness he felt love. Seeing his daughter and grandchildren so happy was the best gift he could receive.

By early evening everybody was full of food, chocolate and cheese. The boys were getting ready for bed and Fred decided it was time to go home. He had had a wonderful day and was pleased he had changed his mind about going.

Upon returning home he recognised his own lack of Christmas decorations.

'I have been extremely un-festive this year.' He said aloud, before turning on the television and allowing the end of a Christmas film to play out in the background. He then went to the attic and found Marie's Christmas box, bringing it back to the living room to inspect. He hung tinsel over various picture frames, and placed festive ornaments on the fireplace. Finally he plugged in the small fiber optic Christmas tree and placed it in the window.

'There…' he said, finally sitting down in his chair with a hot drink, 'Marie would be proud.' Smiling to himself he sipped on his drink and watched the final few minutes of the Christmas film.

It wasn't long until he fell asleep, and his exhausting day caused his snoring to overpower the television that had been left on.

'Fred…' came a voice he recognised, 'can you hear me?'

'Marie?' Fred's voice was hoarse. 'Is that you?' There standing in the bay window was his wife. 'But how?'

'Darling I am so proud of you today, I know it took a lot of strength in you to carry on without me, but I am elated with what you did.' Fred began to cry, his hands stretched out to reach his treasured wife. Marie stretched out her own hand and held his tight.

'Fear no longer my love, I am here for you, I have always been here for you. Now dry your eyes, for I have come for you tonight so that we can be together forever.'

Fun Christmas Facts

THE tradition of putting tangerines in stockings comes from 12th-century French nuns who left socks full of fruit, nuts and tangerines at the houses of the poor.

The Dog Peed on the Christmas Tree

A Poem

He'd been with us for quite some time,
Our little dog that we named Dime.
Just 9 months old to the day was he,
The day we put up our Christmas tree.

A horrid day with wind and hail,
Yet that didn't stop his excited tail.
He ran around the tree full speed,
And ended up stuck in the electric lead.

The baubles he thought were a funny new game,
burying them in the garden without any shame.
But was the fairy that took the biggest of hits,
losing her wings and scattered in bits.

Then the next day his poo sparkled and glimmered,
We realised he'd eaten the tinsel and glitter.
And just when you think things couldn't get worse,
He chewed up the stockings, and made Mother curse.

Then on Christmas Eve when the house was still,
He ate Santa's mince pie off the window sill.
Then he knocked the tree over and dragged it to bed,
And peed on the branches, before resting his head.

When morning arrived Dime was greeted with
laughter,
Then for dinner got turkey, and a bone to chew after.
Then as evening drew in he lay by the fire,
Christmas, he thought, is something to admire.

Fun Christmas Facts

MANY parts of the Christmas tree can actually be eaten, with the needles being a good source of Vitamin C.

BEFORE turkey, the traditional Christmas meal in England was a pig's head and mustard.

Front Line

It had been quite for days now, yet Thomas' ears still rung from the deafening sound of the canons fire. Never in his wildest dreams did he expect it to be as bad as this. It was December 24th 1916, and exactly seven months to the day that he turned 18 years old. His father had tried to warn him what it would be like, his mother tried everything in her power to stop him from going, yet here he was patrolling the trenches somewhere in France.

The journey here had been harsher than he had expected, the constant walking ever since landing in Calais. This wasn't the first trench he had been stationed, the first was much smaller and after weeks of intense gun fire the showdown eventually came to a head when they went over the trenches and into no-mans-land. Strangely for Thomas it wasn't the battle that he found the most overwhelming, but the task of then collecting up the corpse. Men he had spent months with, now lying dead in the field around him, and he had to help remove them.

War was not a game. Recruiters made it sound like an honour to fight for their country, but what real honour is there when you are laid dead in a field?

Thomas wrote regularly to his mother, she had insisted upon it. He was an only child and she worried about him dearly. Her letters were always filled with positivity and hope, praying for his safety, and letting him know what was happening back home. Thankfully for his parents they lived in the country and were relatively safe in the grand scheme of things. His parents were much older than those of people his age, both being in their late fifties.

Thomas hated being on patrol in the trenches, the time always seemed to go so slowly, especially at night time when there was nobody else around. It was still only early in the evening, yet it was already dark. The cold winter wind blew through the trench, causing Thomas to shiver. The uniform he wore was thick and designed for the winter cold, but being exposed to the elements for so many hours at a time made the uniform feel ineffective.

As Thomas walked the length of the trench he occasionally came across one of the other patrolling officers.

'Thomas.' The other solider greeted him as they met.

'Another quiet night ahead, James?'

'Looks that way.' James was much taller than Thomas, he was thin with a long face and long pointed nose; a complete contrast to Thomas who was much more muscular and of average height. 'Be much better when this whole blasted war is over, we can get back to our lives.' James was also much older than Thomas and had children of his own.

'Agreed, the sooner we can all go home the better.' Said Thomas.

'And they said it would be all over before Christmas, yet here we are, hours away from the day in question. If you ask me this is going to go on for even more years to come.' James spoke with a tremble in his voice. He was normally one for keeping the spirits high, but even he was beginning to crack under the constant strain.

Thomas wished James a pleasant evening and returned the way he came. The trenches went on for miles and miles, this was the end of his stretch. It was so narrow in places, and the darkness meant he could barely see more than a couple of feet before him. From time to time he would take a peak over the top, he was supposed to do this as part of his patrol, but in the dark there was nothing ever to be seen. It was so quiet tonight; he couldn't hear anything from the trenches at the other side. If he hadn't known any better he would have believed the enemy to have left already.

Thomas didn't have a watch with him, but he knew it must have been ten o'clock when the next solider came to take over his section.

'Evening Thomas, a cold one tonight again.'

'Freezing, Robert, but the sky is clear so it should be a dry one.'

Thomas made his way back to the bunker, he shared quarters with five other soldiers in a cramped

room. There was little to do in the evenings other than rest, they knew they could be called upon at a moment's notice and so they slept at every opportunity they could. A couple of the men were still up and talking, one of them however was snoring in the corner which amused the men. Thomas changed out of his outdoor uniform and into something less heavy. They all slept in the basic uniform just in case they needed to be up fast, and there was little room to store anything other than the tiny space between the bed and the floor. Most men had a small tin filled with their valuables, only big enough to store any letters they had received and photographs. Thomas would look through this tin every evening. Inside was six letter from his mother, one had arrived every month. He had always replied to her as soon as he could, and his last letter was sent over three weeks ago.

He sat on his tiny bed re-reading the letters his mother had written in her best handwriting. He could quote the letters by heart already, yet holding them in his hand and looking at her writing made him feel closer to them somehow.

A gently tapping on the door startled them all; the solider closest opened it to see who was there. It was an older soldier from the main camp bringing through supplies. He was over double Thomas' age.

'Evening chaps. Nippy out there.' He dropped a large wooden box on the floor filled with food and water. 'Oh I nearly forgot,' he said on his way out, 'post finally arrive this afternoon.' All the men in the bunker suddenly sat up straight, eager to know if they had a new letter from home. 'Thomson, Brown,

Sanders…' He handed out the letters to each man in turn, 'Wright, and Sharp.' All the men in the bunker got a letter, even Sharp who was out on patrol, but there was no letter for Thomas.

'Is there nothing for me Sir?' He asked, trying his best to hide the sadness in his voice.

'Sorry son, that's all I was handed for this bunker. What name is it; I can always check when I get back.'

'Thomas, Sir, Thomas Jones.'

'I'll get them to send it down with the next load of supplies if it's there. Good night all, Merry Christmas.'

'Merry Christmas.' The remaining soldiers replied, all except Thomas. He sat upon his bed watching as his roommates open up their own letters with excitement. There are always tears when letters arrived, the reminder of being away from home and knowing they are just as much missed. The arrival of letters always brought with it the same after effect each time, ten minutes would be spent in silence reading one's own letter, before the room would engage in conversation about what contents were inside. Knowing the men for so long meant that Thomas felt as though he knew their families too and enjoyed hearing the updates they would bring. But tonight he was in no mood to hear what was in those other letters.

It was the longest night in a while, and Thomas could barely sleep through grief. Was he being stupid to be so upset for not receiving a letter?

The morning arrived and there was a strange atmosphere through the trenches. It was Christmas day and nobody knew exactly how they should react to that. Thomas' squad were all his age so this was the first Christmas away from home for them all. For some it was a harder hit than others, and the knowledge of their families celebrating without them was heart breaking. Despite the importance of the day Thomas still had chores to carry out, and was more than happy to get on with them in the hope to busy himself into forgetting the day, and especially forgetting the letters.

It was a miserable cloudy day, and the temperatures had barely reached above freezing by midday. There had been no activity from the enemy trenches in weeks, and moods at Thomas' side were becoming more and more fatigued.

When night fall came they again took it in turns to patrol their area. Thomas was pleased to be away from his roommates, he hadn't realised before just how much discussion took place after letters arrived. With no letter of his own he couldn't help worry about his parents. He knew they lived in the countryside, but that was no guarantee of safety.

This evening, like most evenings he bumped into James along the trench patrol. He knew James as they had trained together back in England; they were both disappointed when they were separated into different squadrons. James left for France weeks before Thomas did, and so it was an unexpected surprise to see him one evening on the same patrol.

'Merry Christmas Thomas,' He said upon seeing his friend.

'A Merry Christmas indeed.'

'Now cheer up chap, things could be worse. Did the post come to your bunker last night too?'

'Yes, but no letter for me.'

'Oh I am sorry mate. I know how important they are. Hopefully the next batch isn't too far away. In the meantime they are doing the rounds with supplies again, I hear there is a little extra something in the crates tonight, being Christmas and all.' James was trying his best to lighten Thomas' mood, but it was doing no good.

They wished each other a good night and turned back the way they came. They usually saw each other multiple times during their patrols, but didn't like to be seen talking for too long. Eventually the next soldier came to relieve Thomas of his duties. He was frozen to the bone, his hands were blue and he could barely feel his numb face. The bunker was not much warmer, but it did keep out the weather, for the most part. The box of supplies had already been delivered when Thomas got back and the men were all enjoying some wine and cake. Nothing posh, but it was certainly the most exciting thing they had been sent in…well, ever.

As Thomas changed one of the soldiers poured him some wine and sliced up a piece of cake.

'Get that down you mate. You look bloody frozen.'

'Thanks, I wish it was a bottle each.' They both laughed.

'Now that may be considered a party, and they wouldn't allow that now would they.' Thomas changed before settling on his bed to enjoy the cake and wine. Most of the men were already tucked up in bed trying to use their blankets to keep warm.

'Oh I nearly forgot to mention,' the young soldier turned back to Thomas, 'he found your letter, must have been left behind by mistake.' He handed over the envelope and Thomas almost snatched it off of him in excitement. The wine and cake were put to the back of his mind as he ripped open the envelope and saw his mother's handwriting. His hands were shaking with excitement and tears were already beginning to form in his eyes causing him to struggle reading. He tried to steady his hand, and wiped away the tears. He focused on the paper, the opening line read. 'To Thomas, Merry Christmas…'

Fun Christmas Facts

DURING the Christmas of 1914 (World War 1), a truce was held between Germany and the UK. They decorated their shelters, exchanged gifts across no man's land and played a game of football between themselves.

Christmas Time

A Poem

Christmas time is full of cheer
Christmas time is full of beer

Christmas time is dark and cold
Christmas cheer will not get old

Christmas dinner is always hot
Christmas pudding serves up a lot

Christmas crackers go with a bang
Christmas carols the children sang

Christmas comes just once a year
Christmas always seems so near

Christmas presents so hard to wrap
Christmas sales snatch like a trap

Christmas time is always fun
Christmas greetings to everyone

Fun Christmas Facts

SANTA hasn't always dressed in red. Pre 1930s there were many different variations of Santa, sporting a variety of different coloured garments and ranging in sizes from big to small. Some people claim the modern day image of Santa Claus was created by Coca-Cola, but this isn't strictly true. The original red-suited Santa became popular in the US and Canada in the 19th century due to the influence of caricaturist and cartoonist Thomas Nast. Coca-Cola commissioned their depiction of Santa in 1931.

The Snowflake Maker

ugustus Frost sat at his desk and sighed. It was littered with piles upon piles of paper, screwed up into balls. It was dark outside now, and the single candle balancing on the edge of his desk was the only light he had. The room, quite small really, with only the one window overlooking the luscious garden to the back of the house. It has the feel of being inside a log cabin with the amount of exposed beams, cladded walls and worn wooden floor. There was only just enough room for the desk and chair.

Augustus had just turned thirty the previous week; he had short dark hair, that was already beginning to grey around the edges, and icy blue eyes. His usual clean shaven faced graced with stubble, a reminder at just how long he had been working. He wore a shirt whiter than the snow caped mountains, and trousers blacker than coal. Smart attire was his usual appearance.

A knock on the door startled him. 'Come in.' He called.

'Here you are!' Came the voice of a friendly woman, 'you shouldn't still be up working at this time of night sweetheart.'

'What time is it mother?'

'It's nearly one in the morning.' His mother was a short woman with tight curly silver hair. She was standing in her dressing gown clutching a brass candlestick holder. 'I saw your light on when I got up. Come along, I'll make you a drink too.'

Augustus followed his mother out of the office and down into a large open kitchen. There were no lights, and so they began to ignite more candles.

'What's keeping you up son?' His mother asked whilst warming some milk.

'It's this snowflake design, I haven't got one yet.'

'Oh love, you've known this day was coming all your life, have you never considered your design?'

'I guess I just always thought I had plenty of time, but now I have a matter of hours.' Augustus let out another loud sigh as he took a seat at the large dining table. His mother joined him with a steaming mug for them both.

'You know snowflakes are not just something that happen by chance Gus,' Gus was the name she had called him since being a child, 'every eldest child of the Frost family has designed their very own unique snowflake, and when the time comes for them to take over the workshop, that snowflake is the first to fall on Christmas Eve during the handing over ceremony.'

'I know the story mum; I got that part. What I don't have is a design.'

'You know your father designed his when he was eighteen. I had known him for a little while by that point. I remember how excited he was to show me. He told me it has come to him in a dream and that every point of it he named after his siblings. If you look closely enough there is a small heart shape in the middle.' She slurped her hot milk before continuing. 'Has Elizabeth ever asked you about your design?' Elizabeth was Augustus' wife. They had been married for a nearly five years.

'Yes, she takes an interest, but she knew I hadn't come up with anything yet. She knew I would probably be late to bed tonight.'

'Well tomorrow is Christmas Eve, and your snowflake is due to fall around six o'clock in the evening. So I suggest you go to bed and rest, tomorrow you will know what to do.' She stood from the table and kissed her son on the forehead. 'Go to bed Gus, I will see you in the morning.' She let herself out, and walked across the courtyard to her own cottage opposite. The small candlelight guiding her way.

Augustus sat there surrounded by candles and watched as his mother disappeared out of sight. The large cuckoo clock on the wall of the kitchen let out a low *Dong* as it reached half past one.

Still not sleepy, and desperate to get the inspiration he needed for the design, Augustus left the house the same way as his mother and crossed the courtyard. He walked past his parents front door and towards a much larger, carved wooden door. It opened with an enormous groan from the rusty hinges. Holding his candle higher he entered the building. He was standing at the beginning of a very long corridor. Multiple doors could be seen along the way leading off to offices and other such rooms. But what made his corridor special was that its walls were lined with frame after frame. There were so many frames at this side of the corridor that none of the wall underneath could be seen. Each frame, A4 size or smaller, contained a single sketch design of a snowflake, with a date and signature of its creator.

Augustus knew the importance of creating his own special design, a design that would be displayed on these walls for future generations to admire. But more than that it was a way of leaving his mark, his own special design which defined his reign of head of the company; not to mention the Frost family. Augustus walked down the corridor slowly, taking in his ancestors work. Eventually he made it to the end of the corridor where bare walls could now be seen. His father's snowflake the last to be framed and mounted.

The door at the end of the corridor led into the workshop. A place that was full of life by day, but by night it was deserted and silent. Everybody knows that elves work in toy workshops, but very few know that pixies work in snowflake workshops. Their small hands ideal for hand carving each and every winter snowflake. The workshop was constantly cold, to preserve the ice that was used to carve out the snowflakes. Each workspace had the same tiny tools for chipping away at the ice, and each pixie had their own designated design to follow; some more complex than others.

Augustus left the workshop, and as he re-crossed the courtyard he stopped for a moment to admire the moon. It was a just a thin curved wafer in the sky surrounded by millions of stars. Tomorrow his father officially steps down as chief snowflake maker, and he takes on the top job, a job he had been training for his entire life. Augustus had helped out in the workshop with his father since he was young, he can even remember his grandfather working there too, and how the hand over period to his father seemed like such a huge celebration at the time.

He returned back to his kitchen and cleaned up the mugs he and his mother had used; before heading back upstairs. For a second he considered returning to his office for another attempt at a design, but a yawn finally persuaded him that it was rest he needed.

His wife Elizabeth was fast asleep, and Augustus undressed quietly before carefully sliding in beside her. Exhausted he fell asleep almost instantly.

Augustus woke before sunlight, his mind again racing at the prospect of the day ahead. He could hear the muffled sound of talking from outside the window; clearly the pixies were arriving to start the day. His wife Elizabeth stirred as her husband leapt from the bed.

'Honey, what time did you make it to bed?' Her voice croaked as she spoke.

'It was nearly two. But I didn't get a design yet so I'm going to get an early start today and make sure it's ready for the ceremony this evening.' Augustus dressed in a hurry, kissed his wife on the lips and shot downstairs. From his kitchen window he could see his father in the courtyard speaking to one of the pixies. She was no bigger than a candle flame, but the fluttering of her wings sent sparks of glittering light out around her.

The courtyard was filled with Pixies all heading for the workshop, their tiny voices together echoed through the courtyard, and the sparks from their wings all together made for an impressive light show.

'Ah Gus, here you are.' His father's voice boomed across the yard at the sight of him. He was a tall man with broad shoulders and a pure white beard and eyebrows. He always wore a checked shirt with the sleeves rolled up, and was never seen without his flat cap on. Augustus used to say he looked like Santa

Claus as a farmer. 'I want to introduce you to Miss Dasilva. She is our newest recruit and will be helping you today make your design.'

'Pleased to meet you miss.'

'Likewise Sir.' She gave a little curtsy.

'Right then,' Mr Frost interrupted, 'I will let the two of you get on, I'm looking forward to seeing the final design tonight.' With that Mr Frost retreated back into his own house, leaving Augustus and Miss Dasilva alone.

'It is an honour to be working for the Frost family,' Miss Dasilva announced, 'my grandmother worked here for the longest of times.'

'We are pleased to have you here. Shall we?' He signalled for them to continue towards the workshop. 'I will give you a quick tour and then we better get down to business.'

'Oh I don't need a tour Sir, Mr Frost already did that the other day, I've been assigned a work area already.'

'Ah…right…okay then. Well I guess we should get on.'

'Do you have the design on you sir? I may need a couple of attempts in perfecting it, but at least we have all day.'

'Erm, well…you see, the thing is…' Augustus stuttered, he could feel his face turning red.

'Please tell me you have a design?' Miss Dasilva looked anxious.

'Not exactly.' He looked at the floor in shame.

'Right then Sir, we need to get you a design and quick. Do you have a pad and pencil?'

'I have one in my office.'

'Go get it and we will take it with us.'

'Take it where?'

'Sir, you know better than me that snowflakes are a thing of beauty, and many of the original designs came from the natural worlds influence. You can't sit in an office and design a snowflake, you need to be outside. A walk in the woods should do it.' Augustus smiled, it wasn't the worse idea, and given his current rate of success it was certainly worth a shot.

'Okay, wait there.' He ran back into the house and grabbed his pad and pencil, returning moments later and finding Miss Dasilva exactly where he had left her.

They left the courtyard and began to walk down the lane towards the local town, but before reaching the town they veered off onto a woodland trail.

'I always loved this place.' Said Augustus. 'The magical creatures here take such care of the woodlands; it is beautiful in every season.

'Many of my family work in the woods,' Miss Dasilva replied, 'they care for the wildflowers and help spread the seed for next year's crop. Winter is now a time for cleaning and getting the woodlands ready for Spring.'

As Augustus walked along the track, and Miss Dasilva flew alongside him, the dense woodlands became quieter and quieter the further the ventured in. 'I recognise this part,' He said, 'if I'm not mistaken...yes there it is.' He was pointing at a small swing hanging from the branch of a tree. 'My brother and I used to come here all the time to play. There

used to be a giant mushroom village here, but I think the Pixies didn't like the footpath being so close to them and they moved away.'

'I'm a little young to remember the village,' Miss Dasilva replied 'but my mother told me all about it. She told me that trolls destroyed the village pillaging for food, the footpath was blamed as it lead them right to the village.'

Augustus sat on the swing and kicked off the ground as hard as he could. His messy hair blew in the breeze and he let out a playful 'Wahoo.' The swing was attached to an old oak tree, one of the tallest trees in the entire woods. Although now completely bare for winter, the brown and orange leaves still littered the base around his feet.

'I have always loved this tree.' Augustus stopped the swing and looked up in admiration. 'We used to climb it and race each other to the top. It's always the most colourful too, the greenest in summer, and the best display of oranges and yellows in October.' Miss Dasilva picked up one of the leaves and brought it over to him, it was over twice her size. She rested it on his knee.

'It sounds to me,' she said slightly out of breathe, 'that this tree has a lot of memories for you.'

'It does indeed.' He admired the leaf and smiled, his thoughts filled with all the fun and laughter it had produced with him and his brother.

'I think Sir, you may have found your inspiration.' Augustus' eyes widened at her words, he looked down at the beautiful golden leaf in his hand and smiled. 'Miss Dasilva, you are a genius.'

With the leaf pressed carefully between the sheets of the sketch pad Augustus and Miss Dasilva took off at speed back towards to the workshop. Upon reaching her workspace they each took a sheet of paper and began to outline ideas using the leaf as inspiration. Ignoring the bustling workshop around them they frantically drew idea after idea. Occasionally showing one and other their drawings, they would then take the parts of each other's they liked and worked it into a more improved version of their own.

'I've got it.' Augustus burst with excitement. He swung the paper around to show Miss Dasilva, who immediately beamed with delight at the drawing.

'Oh Sir,' she said, 'that is a beautiful snowflake if I do say so. I hope I can do it justice when I start carving the ice.'

It was already after lunch, and there was no time to waste. Miss Dasilva brought over an ice block to her working station and began to chip away at it. Augustus watched her anxiously as she glanced back at his drawing every couple of seconds. 'Ahhh!' she suddenly screamed. 'I made a mistake.' She flew off to get another slab of ice, and upon returning she pushed the old piece onto the floor.

'Maybe I made the design too complex,' said Augustus, 'let me simplify it for you to make the carving easier.'

'No!' She shouted, 'Your design is perfect, I just need to concentrate.' She chipped away again and again, and each time throwing it to one side claiming it was not right. When Augustus looked up at the clock again it already read five o'clock; where on earth had the time gone? The ceremony started in less than an hour.

Eventually Miss Dasilva finished one sculpture of Augustus' design. She placed it in a protective clear box and handed it to him. 'Keep it safe until the ceremony, I think I have the technique figured out now so I'll try and make a couple more in time. You go and change.'

'Thank you Miss Dasilva, I hope you're going to be there?'

'I wouldn't miss it Sir.'

Augustus dashed from the workshop, the snowflake box tightly in his hand, and headed back to his bedroom to change. Every Frost family member in history has always worn a pure white suit during the snowflake ceremony, and he had had his suit made especially for the occasion. The shirt, tie, jacket and trousers were all snow white, and he had even had silver shoes made especially.

'There you are,' his wife Elizabeth's voice came through the door, 'I was wondering where you had gotten to.' She was wearing a beautiful floor length sequined gown that was pale blue. She was a tall thin woman with jet black hair and blue eyes that matched her dress.

'Your father has been asking me when you will be ready.' She asked.

'Just one more minute, I am nearly there. Wait for me and I will walk you down.' Augustus tied his shoe laces and was ready. He handed Elizabeth the snowflake box to take a look at and her face lit up with joy.

'Oh darling, it is gorgeous. All the detail throughout really makes it sparkle in the light. It looks like it's made from crystal or diamonds, not ice.' He took her by the hand and led her back down into the courtyard. His mother and father were both there waiting for him. The yard was now lit with hundreds of pixie's hovering around to watch the proceedings.

'Ah my son,' Mr Frost's deep voice called out, 'you are right on time.' He too was wearing a white suit, and his mother a knee length deep blue dress. Augustus handed over the snowflake box to his father, who took it with anticipation. The snowflake had six points, each resembling that of an oak leaf; and joining them in the middle was the most delicately detailed flower.

'Oak leaf?' Mr Frost said breaking the moments silence.

'Yes…yes it is. I can't believe you got that so quickly.'

'It is stunning son, you should be very proud of yourself.' He handed back the box, Augustus was confused to be getting it back.

'Isn't this going off to be the first snowflake of Christmas?'

'No son, this is the first carving of your creation. You keep that for yourself. Miss Dasilva here tells me she had made four more.' Miss Dasilva appeared from behind with a similar box filled with the four snowflakes. Augustus gave her the warmest of smiles. Before they could exchange pleasantries there was a loud Gong from the clock face above the courtyard, it was officially six o'clock.

A beam of light shot down from the sky, and a beautiful lady began to slowly descend. It was Mother Nature. Augustus liked Mother Nature, her appearance changed with every season, and now that winter had arrived she was dressed head to toe in blues and whites. She sparkled as though she had been sprinkled in glitter, even her eyelids sparkled. Her dark skin glowed and her pearl white teeth shone as she smiled.

'Good evening Master Frost,' her tone was calm and collective, 'I would like to be the first to congratulate you on your new position as chief of the snowflake workshop. You are the four hundredth and fifty sixth member of your family to take on the role. I am blessed to have had the honour to meet each and every one. The original Mr Jack Frost would be humbled to see his descendants taking such pride in continuing his legacy. Do you have the new design?' Miss Dasilva came forward and handed Mother

Nature the small box containing the four little flakes. She held the box closer to her face to examine them, a smile telling Augustus that she approved.

'Good evening Mother Nature,' Mr Frost interjected before she left, 'please do call in for a longer visit some time, it has been years.'

'Thank you Thomas, I agree it has been a long time. But for now I must go, as you know Mister Claus won't set off until he has the cover of snow fall. Augustus, good luck again; and a very Merry Christmas to you all.' The beam of light brightened and Mother Nature began to rise up into the air. The courtyard was silent as they watched her ascend back up into the sky, the swish of hundreds of pixies wings the only sound. As the beam of light faded and eventually disappeared they all continued to look up to the sky, waiting patiently for any sign of the first snowfall. They didn't have to wait long, as a singular snowflake began to float down from the sky into the yard. There was no mistaking it was one of Augustus'. The Frost family and the hundreds of pixies watched in silence as it fell to the ground, and upon reaching the cobbled ground the pixies began to cheer and scream with excitement. The cheers soon turned to hugging and wishing one and other a Merry Christmas. Augustus' parents rushed to his side and scooped him up into a group hug, his wife Elizabeth quickly joining in.

'Thank you everybody.' He spoke to the courtyard as the snow began to fall faster, 'but especially thank you to Miss Dasilva, I couldn't have done it without you.' Miss Dasilva blushed.

'Thank you Mr Frost, Sir; and a Merry Christmas to you.'

Snowflake by Augustus Frost

Original Snowflake
By Jack Frost

Snowflake By
Thomas Frost
(Augustus's Dad)

Other Notable Frost Family Designs:

Fun Christmas Facts

THE people of Oslo, Norway donate the Trafalgar Square Christmas tree every year in gratitude to the people of London for their assistance during WWII.

Christmas Game!

Can you solve the picture puzzles to reveal the 4
hidden Christmas related word.

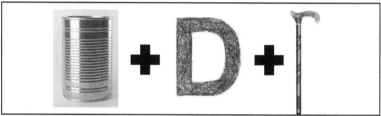

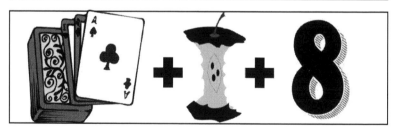

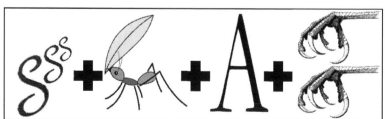

Let's Build A Snowman

Let's go build a snowman,
my best friend said to me.
Let's make him tall and friendly,
and let's build him by the tree.

I'd love to build a snowman,
I replied to my best friend
We should get to work quite quickly
for he'll need a large rear end.

We rolled up snow in ball shapes
until we couldn't roll no more
we pushed them round the garden
until our hands and feet were sore.

We worked on through the chill
the cold wind biting at our nose.
Then went inside to warm up,
returning with some clothes.

On his head we placed a hat
he looked so smart already
then a bright red scarf around his neck
and a coat to cover his belly.

We used two branches for his arms
and gloves to keep him warm
he looks so warm and toasty
fit to face the next snowstorm.

"Do you think that we should name him"
I asked me friend excited
"What about Sir Frosty Pants?"
and then he can be knighted

Night time brought a raging storm
Melting poor Frosty, right away.
"Don't worry" I said "we can always re-build
On the next cold snowy day."

Fun Christmas Facts

HANGING stockings out comes from the Dutch custom of leaving shoes packed with food for St Nicholas's donkeys. He would leave small gifts in return.

Reindeer Delivery

I t was just a week until the big day, and Santa Claus and his elves were busy making final plans. Mrs Claus checked all the gifts were being wrapped with a big bow before being placed into the sack, and the elves were cleaning up the sleigh for the journey ahead.

Santa was in his office, sipping a hot coco. He was reading the naughty and nice list for the second time.

'More and more on the naughty list.' He said with a sigh. The list would take him a couple of days to get through, and he needed to make sure no mistakes were made. Suddenly there was a knock on the door. 'Come in.' Santa shouted, and the door creaked open.

'Excuse me Sir, but we have an issue.' It was Otis, the head reindeer handler. He was barely four feet tall, yet he was still one of the tallest elves at the North Pole.

'What is it Otis, I have a lot of work to do.'

'I know sir, but I thought you should know that we have had to split up Donner and Blitzen.' Santa put down his mug of coco and turned to face Otis, his face filled with concern.

'Why? What has happened?'

'Well sir, Donner has been unwell for a couple of days now. We thought it may be just a twenty four hour bug, but he is still unwell. I have moved Blitzen away in the hope he doesn't catch anything.'

'Will he be well enough to fly next week?' Santa asked with worry.

'I'm not sure. He needs to rest for now and we can decide in the next couple of days.'

'Thank you Otis, you may

go.' Santa returned to his naughty and nice list, he was in no mood to read it now and instead downed the coco in one gulp and left his office. He bumped into Mrs Claus in the doorway.

'I was just coming to see you dear.' She said in her typical jolly voice.

'Have you heard about Donner?' Santa asked her.

'No, what is the matter?' He explained what had happened to her on the way. They went down to the stables where Otis could be found talking to the reindeer, he hadn't heard them come in.

'Now, now Donner. Come on you need to eat something, get your strength back.'

'He does look a little paler than usual.' Said Santa, causing Otis to jump.

'Yes sir. I am trying to encourage him to eat, but he isn't interested.' Mrs Claus entered the stable and sat next to Donner in the hay.

'Now then,' she said, stoking his head, 'let us have a think what we can make you. Nobody wants normal food when they are unwell.'

'How is Blitzen? Santa asked Otis.

'He seems fine sir, nothing out of the ordinary. It's just Donner who is showing signs of ill health.'

'I want a daily report,' Said Santa, 'I want to know how he is doing. I think given his condition and that we are due to fly in six days that maybe he should stay grounded this time.'

'I agree sir.' Santa left the stables and left Otis and Mrs Claus to nurture the sick animal.

'Otis have you examined Donner at all to try and determined what the issue may be?'

'No Miss, we have never had a sick reindeer before, I don't know what to look for.' Mrs Claus tried to give the animal a look over, but being laid down in the hay made it very difficult indeed.

'Otis,' said Mrs Claus, 'I have never really been this close to the reindeer, but I think I can spot something that may be the cause of his...or should I say her sickness.'

'Her?' Questioned Otis. 'But all the reindeer are male, except Cupid of course?'

'How long have Donner and Blitzen been sharing the large stable?'

'Erm, quite a while now, it was just until the

leak in the roof was fixed; four or five months maybe?'

'Well Otis I believe we are going to have another reindeer in the herd.' Otis looked at Mrs Claus with a puzzled expression. 'I better go tell my husband the news.'

Mrs Claus returned to find her husband snoozing by the fire, the naughty and nice list on his lap.

'Dear, are you awake?' She gave his shoulder a little nudge.

'Huh?...oh yes, quite. What is it?' He sat up in his chair trying to pretend he was never asleep.

'You will be pleased to know that Donner is going to be just fine. However she will not be flying this Christmas Eve.'

'Oh well I suppose it is for the best that he rests...hold on, what did you say, She?'

'Yes, Donner is a girl, and furthermore she is having a baby.'

'Goodness me. How did we not know she was a girl before?'

'I think darling, Otis is a good reindeer handler, but he is not very good when it comes to anything else. She has been sharing a stable with Blitzen for the first time, and well...you know.'

'Ah, I see.' Santa was a little lost for words. 'Well never mind, how long do you think until she gives birth?'

'Looking at her, I'd say any day.'

Christmas Eve had finally arrived. Santa was in his room getting into his warm red suit and boots when there was a knock at the door.

'Come in.' He shouted, expecting it to be Mrs Claus, but it wasn't, it was Otis.

'Santa I'm here to let you know that the remaining seven reindeer are all harnessed to the sleigh and ready for you. Also Donner just went into labour.' He turned to leave.

'Wait!' Santa hollered at him. 'Where is my

wife?'

'Mrs Claus is in the stable with Donner, I am going back there myself now to assist.'

'Okay, well I need to leave, but I will come straight to the stable upon my return.' Santa left his room and headed for the departure runway, he didn't really want to leave his wife alone with Donner but he knew he needed to leave straight away otherwise he would never get his deliveries finished in time.

Santa loved Christmas Eve, it was the day when all the years hard work came to an end. Yet despite the successful trip, he couldn't take his mind off of Donner.

The North Pole was quiet when he returned. It was Christmas day, and the elves were always quieter after spending Christmas Eve partying. As usual Otis met Santa to help return the reindeer to the stables, he didn't say anything about Donner and Mrs Claus and so Santa headed though to see them himself. Upon entering the stables Mrs Claus instantly shushed him.

'Not too loud,' she whispered, 'Olive has just

taken her first steps.'

'Olive?' He queried.

'She has deep green eyes,' she replied, 'I thought it suited her. Santa leaned passed his wife to get a better view. Donner was on her feet, and below her was a tiny little reindeer stretching up to its mother to feed.

'It's been a while since we had a baby of any kind here.' Santa commented, watching Olive with admiration. 'Well little one, welcome to the North Pole.'

Fun Christmas Facts

JAMES Pierpont's 1857 song Jingle Bells was first called One Horse Open Sleigh and was originally written for Thanksgiving.

The Truth
A Poem

Old Saint Nick is a cleaver old man
When he devised a devilish plan
To fool the people of the Earth
With small white lies of enormous worth

The North Pole he would let you believe
Was home to his workshop and personal retrieve
But truth be told this is not right
For up there they would get frostbite

Those rosy red cheeks are not from cold
But sunburn, or at least that's what I've been told
The cookies and milk consumed once a year
Then the rest of the time it's seafood and beer

The reindeer bathe in the tropical ocean
Whilst Mrs Claus rubs her shoulder with lotion
And the elves have a great time climbing the trees
For coconuts and honey direct from the bees

So whilst you're all searching for him through the
snow
Santa is warm in his beach bungalow
He'll pose for your pictures in snow covered scenes
Then return home to paradise, a land of dreams

Fun Christmas Facts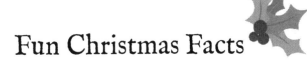

BOXING Day is not named because of all the boxes and garbage to be disposed of, but in fact gets its name from all the money collected in church alms-boxes for the poor.

The Many Names for Santa

Country	Name
Belgium	Pere Noel
Brazil	Papai Noel
Chile	Viejo Pascuero ("Old Man Christmas")
China	Dun Che Lao Ren ("Christmas Old Man")
Netherlands	Kerstman
Finland	Joulupukki
France	Pere Noel
Germany	Weihnachtsmann ("Christmas Man")
Hawaii	Kanakaloka
Hungary	Mikulas (St. Nicholas)
Italy	Babbo Natale

Japan	Hoteiosho (a god or priest who bears gifts)
Norway	Julenissen ("Christmas gnome")
Poland	Swiety Mikolaj (St. Nicholas)
Russia	Ded Moroz ("Grandfather Frost")
Sweden	Jultomten ("Christmas brownie")
United Kingdom	Father Christmas / Santa Claus

Fletcher & Hugo

Fletcher put the finishing touches to his snowman; he had managed to find some coal for the eyes, a crooked carrot for the nose, and his father's old flat cap and scarf.

'There, finished.' He admired his work with such pride. Fletcher was seven years old and lived with his two fathers and their cat, Tiddles. It was a small house, with just two bedrooms, and a tiny garden that Fletcher enjoyed playing in. So small was the garden that he had had to collect more snow for his snowman from the park opposite his house.

'Come inside soon son,' his father's voice called from the kitchen, 'it's getting dark.'

'Okay dad.' Fletcher replied. He took one last longing look at his work before turning to head inside.

'Psst.' Came a voice from beyond the fence at the bottom of the garden, 'are you there?' It was Hugo, the kid who lived in the house whose garden backed onto their own.

'Oh, hi Hugo.' Fletcher responded.

'Been building a snowman Fletch? You should have said, we could have built an army of them in my garden.' Hugo's house and garden were much larger than Fletchers. Although they were the same age they went to very different schools, Fletcher attended the local Church of England around the corner, whereas Hugo attended the academy school at the other side of town. The boys had grown up together as garden neighbours, and as most of Hugo's school friends lived across town his mother always arranged playdates with Fletcher.

'Have you been building snowmen today too?' Asked Fletcher.

'No, not today. Our school only finished for the Christmas break today, mother has made me finish all my homework this evening so I can enjoy the rest of the time off. Did you get much homework?'

'A little, but I'll do it just before going back.'

'Want to go to the park tomorrow with my football?' Hugo asked with anticipation.

'Sure. See you tomorrow then.' Fletcher ran off back towards his house. He liked Hugo, but only for short periods of time. He used to hate the forced playdates their parents would set up for them, thankfully they had become rarer ever since starting school, but occasionally they would randomly arrange another.

'Was that Hugo's voice I heard?' His father, Michael, asked as soon as he walked through the door. He was a tall skinny man with short hair that was always styled into a quiff at the front. He always wore a t-shirt with a funky pattern on, and a smarter shirt over the top with jeans.

'Yes, he invited me to the park tomorrow with him.'

'That will be nice. I haven't seen his mother in a while; no doubt she will invite us around for a Christmas drink again.' Michael worked at the school as the music teacher, and so he and Fletcher always spent the holidays together. Fletcher's other dad, Nick, worked as an accountant in the city.

'Is dad not home yet?' Fletcher asked, as his father Michael served them up a portion of homemade lasagne.

'He had a meeting in London today champ, so it's just us two for dinner. He should be home before you go to bed though.' Fletcher dived into his dinner as though he hadn't eaten in months. Constructing a snowman had built him up an appetite. After dinner he helped his dad clear away the dishes, and then ran through into the living room to put the Christmas tree lights on. Their terrace house had a small bay window, and in it they had decorated a six foot artificial tree. Fletcher was the one who put on the lights; it was his favourite part of the day. He would often sit and watch as the lights changed colour.

By nine o'clock his other father was still not home, and so he got himself ready for bed. He had some new pyjamas that had a Harry Potter symbol on the chest, and as he brushed his teeth he heard the front door slam. Fletcher rushed to finish and charged back downstairs, and into the kitchen where he found his other dad taking off his coat.

'Your back!' He hollered with excitement. 'How was London?'

'Hey young man, you should be in bed. London was rainy, but I still managed to get you something.' Nick replied. He was equally as tall as his husband Michael, but was more muscular. His broad shoulders made him look as though he should be a rugby player, and his strawberry blonde hair flopped down over his ears in his usual wind swept appearance.

'What is it? What it is?' Fletcher clapped with excitement. Nick returned to his shoulder bag and pulled out a paper wrapped item.

'I wonder what it could be.' Nick jokingly said as he handed it over. Fletcher immediately ripped open the packaging to reveal a comic book.

'Oh yes!' He screamed, 'new Avengers. Thank you dad.' He gave his father a tight hug before rushing out of the kitchen and up the stairs.

'Twenty minutes Fletch and I want lights out.' Nick laughed as he spoke.

'You know he won't sleep now with excitement.' Michael sniggered, 'Your trips are becoming an expectation of treats.'

'Well if you disapprove, maybe I won't give you your gift?' Michael smirked.

'Now, now…let's not be hasty.' Nick took out a small box from his bag and handed it to Michael. Inside was a pocket watch, but not just any pocket watch, it was Michaels grandfathers pocket watch.

'I had it repaired for you.' Said Nick. 'It had stopped working so long ago and I know you have been wanting it back to working condition forever.'

Michael smiled and pulled his partner in for a warm embrace.

'Thank you, it's perfect.'

The next day was Saturday, and at ten o'clock in the morning there was a knock on the door. It was Hugo, he was carrying his football under his arm.

'Is Fletch in Sir?' He asked Michael.

'Fletch!' He called back into the house, 'Hugo's here for you!' Within seconds Fletcher came hurtling down the stairs.

'I just need to put my boots on.' He told Hugo as he began searching in the cupboard under the stairs.

'You two don't go far.' Michael told them before returning to the kitchen. The park was only across the street from their house, and Michael usually kept an eye on them both from the living room window.

'Come on Fletch, hurry up.' Hugo's voice was quite posh in comparison to Fletcher's and even his clothing was much more expensive. The two boys darted across the road and into the park. It was a huge park that was split into many sections. The playing fields were closest to Fletchers house, and beyond was the boating lake. There was also a woodlands in the park, and Japanese garden, and a play area at either end of the park each with a coffee shop. The two boys barely ever left the playing fields, with its large open area to kick a football around, and the surrounding trees for climbing. In the summer it was fun to watch the boating lake and laugh at the people trying to row.

Today the park was covered in a white blanket of snow, this made it difficult to play one on one football. They contemplated making snowmen instead, but it resulted in them having a snowball fight. The park was strangely quiet for a Saturday, a few dog walkers passed by as the morning drew on, but there wasn't anybody else playing in the fields.

'They are probably all in the coffee shop keeping warm.' Said Hugo. 'My mum often goes to the one on the north side of the park with my grandma. She prefers it because it overlooks the Japanese garden.'

'Yeah but the cakes are better at the coffee shop on the south side.' Fletcher interjected.

The boys returned to Fletchers house for lunch where Michael had made them soup.

'This will keep you boys going in this cold weather.' He said to them. 'Are you playing out again this afternoon?'

'Certainly.' Hugo answered, dunking his crusty bread into the soup. When they had finished they both thanked him for the soup and returned to the park as quickly as they could.

The afternoon turned cloudy and fresh snowstorms had been forecast. The boys had left the football behind this time. They made their way to the play area, but apart from a couple of teenagers it was empty. The coffee shop nearby however looked to be full. Beyond the coffee shop was a small stone bridge, a little stream passed underneath. They stopped and leaned against the side for a moment and watched the water as it flowed quickly below. Hugo picked up a fallen branch from the ground and threw it into the stream. They both then watched as the current took it under the bridge. As it disappeared out of sight they raced to the opposite side of the bridge to see it come out the other end.

'Let me get a branch too,' said Fletcher, 'and we can see who's comes out first.' The pair of them searched nearby for the perfect branch, before again standing in the centre of the bridge.

'One…two…drop!' Hugo shouted. The branches both landed in the water at similar times, and as soon as they went under the bridge they raced to the other side to see who had won.

'I win, I win.' Hugo cheered. 'I am the champion branch racer.'

'Okay, okay, you win; but how about best of three?' Fletcher challenged his friend.

'You're on!' Again they searched for a stick, and repeated their game, this time Fletcher coming out as victorious.

'It all rests on the final stick.' Fletcher teased Hugo. He knew Hugo was competitive, and when it came to Hugo so was Fletcher. They released their final sticks into the water, and upon seeing Fletchers appear first from the other side, Hugo began to sulk. He picked up a large rock and threw it into the water as hard as he could, which created an almighty splash.

'Do you mind!' a voice came from under the bridge. Both boys froze and looked at one another in shock. They leaned over the bridge, but couldn't see anybody.

'Who do you think it is?' Fletcher whispered to his friend.

'I don't know, but I think we should leave.'

'No, let's go down and take a look.' Fletcher was already headed for the slope that leads down to the water's edge.

'Fletch, no, what if it's somebody dangerous.' Hugo's voice sounded scared. But Fletcher wasn't listening and continued down the slope as quietly as he could. When he reached the bottom he peered around the bottom of the bridge, and sat underneath it was a large man with a long grey beard. He was dressed in what looked like a sleeping bag and was using a rucksack as a pillow.

'Go away.' He shouted, catching Fletcher spying on him. Fletcher didn't have to be told again and raced back up the banking to where Hugo was waiting.

'Well?' Hugo asked, all the while encouraging Fletcher to get away from the bridge.

'It was an old man. He was just sitting there.'

'Why would he do that?' Hugo asked, 'Surely its warmer in the coffee shop, or at home.'

'Maybe he doesn't have a home.' Fletcher replied, 'maybe he lives in the park and we never knew.'

'Well that's the last time I'm going near the bridge.' Claimed Hugo.

Over the next couple of days Fletcher couldn't stop thinking about the man under the bridge. He occasionally saw Hugo, and each time he mentioned the man Hugo had told him to stop talking about it.

On Christmas Eve Fletcher returned to the bridge alone. Standing on the bridge he couldn't see or hear the man below, was he still there? His train of thought was cut short when the sound of women laughing came from the entrance of the nearby coffee shop. Fletcher knew he shouldn't be this far into the park unaccompanied, but he couldn't stop thinking of the man out here alone. Slowly he made his way back down the bank to the waters side, and quietly peered around the corner to catch a glimpse. The old man was still there, only this time he was fast asleep.

Fletcher returned home as quickly as he could, he wanted to tell his dads all about the man, but after running all the way home he could barely get out the words.

'Calm down Fletch,' his father Nick told him, 'and breathe; sit down and tell me what it is you're trying to say.' His other dad Michael came down the stairs. Fletcher was too anxious to sit down.

'What is all this commotion?' He asked with a slight sarcasm in his tone.

'There is a man living in the park, under the bridge by the south point coffee shop.' Both his dads looked at one and other, unsure exactly where this was leading.

'Son, come and take a seat.' Nick spoke, encouraging Fletcher into the living room. The three of them sat on the sofa, a slight hesitation in them all.

'When did you see this man Fletch?' Asked Michael.

'Me and Hugo saw him a couple of days ago, he's living under the bridge. He's still there now.'

'Fletch, you know there are many people in the city that are homeless and live outside, even in winter. It's sad when you see them I know.'

'Isn't there anything we can do for him?' it was clear to his dads that Fletcher wasn't going to let this go.

'Okay son,' Said Nick, 'after dinner how about we plate up the remaining meat and vegetables and take him a portion? Would that be alright?'

'Yes!' Fletcher cheered, 'let's do that.' Dinner was a roasted lamb made by Michael, there were crisp roast potatoes and even Yorkshire puddings, which Fletcher requested with every roast dinner because he loved them so much. Before they could wash the dishes Fletcher was already putting on his boots and coat.

'Come on, come on.' He demanded. Michael packed the dinner into a sealable dish and put it in a carrier bag with some cutlery, napkin and a bottle of water. It was dark now, and the park looked like a completely different place than during the day. The cute Victorian style lamps that lined the pathway gave off very little light. Fletcher led the way, holding onto Nicks hand the entire way he marched them through the park, past the now closed coffee shop, and towards the stone bridge.

'He's under there.' Fletcher whispered. The three of them carefully made their way down the dirt track towards the water's edge. Nick took the lead and as soon as they reached the bottom they saw the elderly man fast asleep. Nick loudly cleared his throat in the hope to wake the man, but he continued to doze.

'Excuse me.' He said, his voice was much deeper than Michaels and under the bridge it echoed. The sleeping man awoke with a fright.

'Who are you, what do you want?'

'We mean you no harm sir,' Nick took the lead, 'my son here saw you were sleeping here and wished for you to have this.' The elderly man looked puzzled, as he was handed over the carrier bag. The smell of warm food filled his nostrils and his face lit up with delight.

'It's lamb, vegetables and potatoes,' Michael piped up, 'I hope you like it.' The elderly man looked speechless as he unwrapped the food and water.

'Thank you young man. You have a kind heart.' Fletcher beamed with delight that the gentleman liked his dinner.

'Is there anything else we can do for you sir,' asked Nick, 'it is Christmas eve after all, you shouldn't be out in the cold alone.'

'You have done more than I could have ever hoped for.' The gentleman replied. 'Now get that young boy of yours home and back into the warmth.'

'Merry Christmas to you.' Nick replied.

Merry Christmas.' Both Fletcher and Michael followed suit.

'Thank you, and to you gents too.'

The three of them returned home, Fletcher didn't like the fact the elderly man was still out in the cold, but he did feel much happier knowing he had a warm meal. Upon returning home they finished clearing away the dishes and settled in for the night watching a Christmas film.

The next morning Fletcher and his dads woke up in the most excitable of moods. It was Christmas day and they always lit the wood burning fire first to warm the house, make hot drinks and toast, and then settle down in the living room to exchange gifts. Each year they would go to one of Fletchers grandparents houses for Christmas dinner, this year it was Nicks parents. Back in his bedroom Fletcher could see from his window that Hugo was in his own back garden. Fletcher ran down the stairs and through the kitchen door all the way to the bottom of his garden where her shouted his friend through the fence.

'Merry Christmas Hugo.'

'Merry Christmas Fletch, did you get good gifts?'

'I got some more comics, a new game and clothes; oh and my auntie gave me £10.' Hugo scuffed at the gifts and began to reel off a list of things he had been bought, all high tech items or expensive pieces of clothing, the list seemed never ending.

'Oh and I got nearly £100 in cash too.' Fletcher rolled his eyes at his friends bragging. He told his friend about giving the homeless man a hot meal, but Hugo seemed less than impressed.

'We are going to my Grans soon,' Fletcher interrupted, 'but before we go I was going to go into the park and give my £10 to the man under the bridge.'

'Why on earth would you do that?' Hugo scoffed. 'That would leave you with no Christmas money left.'

'Well I was thinking he could use it for something he needed.' Fletcher defended himself. 'I was going to invite you along Hugo.'

'Well you needn't bother, because I won't be coming. I'm not giving my Christmas money to somebody who lives under a bridge.'

'Fine.' Fletcher replied, and returned to his house without saying anything more. He had already told his dads what he wanted to do, and they simply smiled and agreed to take him back. So a few hours later as they set off in the car to his Grandmothers, they made a quick diversion towards the coffee shop. Being Christmas day the shop was closed, and so Nick followed his son down onto the banking, leaving Michael in the car waiting. Snow had begun to fall again making the park look picturesque in its fresh coat of white. Fletcher was excited to give the man a gift, and this time lead the way to the base of the bride. Upon reaching the bottom he froze, the elderly man was not there. There was no trace he had ever been there other than the carrier bag with the now empty dish and cutlery they had brought him the night before.

'But where would he have gone?' Asked Fletcher, a touch disappointed.

'Don't be too disheartened Fletch,' Nick scooped him up into a hug, 'what you did yesterday was probably the nicest gesture he had experienced in the longest of time. Not many people would do something as great as what you did.' Fletcher grinned from ear to ear. 'Come, let's get back to the car, your Gran will be wondering where we are.'

The elderly man never returned to the bridge; however Fletcher couldn't resist looking every now and again, just in case.

Fun Christmas Facts

CAROLS began as an old English custom called wassailing, toasting neighbours to a long life.

CAROLS weren't sung in churches until they were introduced by St Francis of Assisi in the 13th century.

New Year's Eve

A Poem

Another year is ending
a new one about to start
I wished I 'd done more things this year
that warmed and melt my heart

Sat with a cup of coco
watching Big Ben on my screen
when did I turn so boring
sat here eating jelly beans

I used to go to parties
and see in the new year drunk
but now I'm turning boring
a couch potato chunk

The new year brings in hope
for a brighter year to come
with resolutions and goals to make
I should probably make some

The chimes of Big Ben echo
midnight is here at last
then memories of the last year
they hit me thick and fast

Auld Lang Syne is sung
I laugh at those who stutter
for who knows all the words anyway
most people they just mutter

The fireworks they light the Thames
a spectacle to behold
the streets are filled with people
that all look freezing cold

And so a new year has arrived
I hope for good things ahead
but for now I'm bloody shattered
and I'm going off to bed

OxqA - ABOUT THE AUTHOR

Luke Bateman is 13 year's old and lives with his mum, dad and older brother in Doncaster, South Yorkshire. Luke enjoys reading and writing he has had his work published in two books.

Luke is now heading towards his GCSES and enjoys playing football in his spare time. Luke's favourite subjects at school are English, mathematics and sport.

A message from Chris:

I would like to thank Luke for creating his story OxqA especially for this book. Luke has a great imagination and I wish him all the best in his writing.

OxqA

By Luke Bateman

It was a cold December day and Kyle was sat in his bedroom doing the last bits of homework before the Christmas break. He was seventeen and just a few months into his A-Levels, he was studying English Literature. His phone beeped, it was a message from his older brother Jordan. Kyle and his brother use to be inseparable when they were kids however Jordan moved to Los Angeles in search of a new career, and was very rarely home anymore.

Later that day Kyle's parents called him downstairs and told him that they had a big surprise for him.

'We have some exciting news.' His mother

said, smiling from ear to ear.

'What is it?' Asked Kyle desperate to know. His parents explained that they were taking him to LA for the holidays and they were going to stay with his brother for Christmas.

'Thanks to my Christmas bonus,' his dad said, 'we can finally afford to visit.' Kyle was so excited he could hardly wait and dashed back upstairs in search of what he wanted to take along. They weren't going for another week, but he was too excited.

The big day finally arrived. Kyle had never been so excited in his life. The drive from the house to the airport was only half an hour, but it seemed like an extremely long time. The plane was on time and they were soon boarding; Kyle managed to get a window seat overlooking the right wing, his dad sat next to him and his mother in the aisle seat.

The flight was long, and every hour that passed seemed longer than the last. Kyle had a book, and a handheld gaming devise, but the small screen on the back of the seats was entertaining him so far.

Halfway into the flight the captain's voice

came over the tannoy. He asked that all passengers return to their seat and secure their seatbelts. Kyle's mum had been to the toilet and was returning when the announcement was made, but before she reached her seat the airplane began to experience some unexpected turbulence. Kyle looked out of the window and saw thick black smoke coming from the wing. He couldn't see how much damage there was, or what may have caused it, but it was clearly the cause of the turbulence. Kyle's heart was in his mouth, he did not know what to do, and just then the cabin lights went out and the oxygen masks were deployed. Screams of fear could be heard throughout the plane, and without warning the airplane began to lose hight at speed.

'Brace, brace, brace!' The captain screamed.

The next thing Kyle remembered was his father tapping him on the shoulder.

'Come on son, we need to go.' The airplane was in darkness, the light from outside flooding in enough for Kyle to follow his dads lead. The craft was being evacuated, and it wasn't until he was in the doorway that Kyle realised they had landed on water.

The passengers were oddly silent, and one by one they descended down the inflatable slide into the inflatable boat.

There was land not too far away, and the boat managed to get all passengers and crew onto dry land. It was nearly sunset, and the beach was deserted. Everybody was beginning to panic, but the Captain reassured them all that he had managed to send off the distress signal just before landing. This didn't seem to comfort some people who began to shout at him.

Kyle and his parents stood back from the commotion, a feeling of hopelessness between them.

Suddenly there was an almighty bang, a pistol had been fired. The passengers all went silent as the silhouettes of men began to appear within the tree line.

As they came out into the fading sunlight it became clear that these were not ordinary men, for they looked to be half machine. They each carried weapons and formed a perfect line against the trees where they just stopped.

Another man appeared between the robotic men, he looked more human. Although he wore on his face a clear mask that was obviously helping him to breathe.

'Good afternoon,' he said, smiling at the passenger, 'my name is Adam and I am so pleased to see visitors.'

'Where are we?' The captain asked, stepping forward from the crowd.

'Ah, you are the one responsible for landing here I presume. Well no worries, we have plenty of room for you all. However before we go, you will all need to place on one of these face masks.'

'May I ask why?' The captain said.

'Now listen up all of you,' Adam completely ignored the captain and addressed the rest of the passengers. 'This island is not safe. After sunset the island releases a bacterium known as Klebsiella pneumoniae, which is typically found in the normal flora of the mouth, skin, and intestines. However this island is unique as the bacteria is slightly different and contains a gene known as OxqA. It can cause destructive changes to human and animal lungs if inhaled.' The passengers all began to mumble between themselves, the sun was setting fast, they were running out of time. Adam instructed his robotic men to hand out the face masks.

'I don't trust this,' Kyles dad whispered to his wife, Kyle overheard.

'What are we supposed to do?' His mum whispered back.

'We have a face mask, we should run for cover.'

'Are you crazy, we could never outrun those robotic men?' Kyle and his parents watched as the passengers all began to leave the beach and follow the robotic army through the trees.

'I call them my OxqA army.' They overheard Adam telling people.

The OxqA army slowly began to disperse as

they escorted the passengers off of the beach.

'Now's our chance.' Dad hissed. He grabbed Kyle by the arm and dragged him along the beach. It didn't take long for the OxqA to spot him, and Adam ordered his soldiers to capture them. Two large robotic men took chase along the sandy beach. Kyle's dad pushed him forward to help him escape. The robotic men caught his mum first, and instead of chasing Kyle and his dad escorted her back to Adam.

'You idiots.' Adam screamed, 'You were supposed to grab all of them, not one.'

Kyle and his dad ran through the trees as fast as they could. Neither dared look back. They began to tire and their running turned to walking.

'I think we lost them.' His dad said.

'But they got mum!' Kyle replied. Their voices distorted through the oxygen masks. They continued walking in the dark until they came to a hut they slowly walked to the hut and opened the door to see no one inside the only thing he saw was a bag and a bed.

'We may be able to rest here for a while,' his dad said, but I wouldn't be surprised if the owner comes back eventually.' They searched the hut, there was only a single bed; but under it lay a bag with a note saying "You will need this" Kyle opened the bag to find a knife and gun with two bullets inside. He showed his father and they both looked at one and other in shock.

Kyle and his father rested for a while, but they knew they couldn't stay there forever. They needed food and water, not to mention they had to save mum.

It was late when they eventually left the hut, and after a short walk they came to a waterfall, the pool of water below sparkled in the moon light. Kyle's dad approached the waterside first, dipping in his fingers to see if it was safe, quickly he loosened his mask and tasted the water dripping from his fingers.

'It's pure.' He said, 'We should be fine to drink it.' Worried about being exposed to the bacteria they scooped up only a couple of handfuls each before returning the masks to their face.

On they walked until a bright light ahead caught their attention, it was the OxqA army headquarters. A large glass building that looked more like a scientists laboratory. Through the glass Kyle and his dad could see Adam and his OxqA army; the army was surrounding the passengers who were all now tied up.

'I knew he wasn't being honest about something.' Kyles dad moaned, 'I wouldn't be surprised if they plan on creating more of those robot monsters.'

'We need to get some help.' Said Kyle.

Kyle and his dad returned to the hut they had found a few hours ago. They camped in the hut overnight, neither of them sleeping as their minds tried to come up with a plan.

They woke the morning to the sound of birds. Daylight gave the island a completely different atmosphere. Hesitantly Kyle and his dad removed their masks, Adams words about it only being dangerous after sunset still clear in their minds.

They left the hut and began their hike back towards the OxqA headquarters. However everything now looked different in the daylight and instead of walking into the woods, they ended up back on the beach.

'Look.' Shouted Kyle. 'A boat.' His dad scanned the water, and low there was indeed a boat drifting just off shore. They both dived into the water and swam towards it. It was a motorboat, so they could use it to go find help. Once they got on the boat they started to look around for someone to help them. The boat was empty, and even worse the pull cord engine wouldn't start. Just then two OxqA robots appeared on the beach, they stood perfectly still as they watched Kyle and his father.

'What are we going to do?' Asked Kyle, his eyes fixed on the OxqA.

'We need to get to Adam, he controls them, so

its him we need to stop.' Kyle nodded in agreement.

'That means we need to be captured,' said Kyle, 'and we can use the knife and gun on Adam.'

'Exactly.' Kyle and his dad returned to the shore. The two OxqA men grabbed them immediately and dragged them back to the lab. Entry to the lab was only permitted by using an eye scanner, and both OxqA scanned themselves before the door slid open.

There was no sign of his mum, or the other passengers. Kyle and his dad were placed in a locked cell and left for what seemed like hours. Eventually the two OxqA returned and dragged Kyle and his dad out of the cell and into a large oval room. The walls were high, but above the walls were rows upon rows of seating, it was almost like they were in a bull fighting ring. The slamming of a door high above them made them jump. It was Adam, and without acknowledging them he walked the perimeter of the ring before taking a seat.

'I am aware that you will want to fight.' Adam spoke, 'You have been trouble ever since you arrived on this island.'

'What is it you want with us?' Kyle screamed at him with anger. Adam laughed.

'A long time ago my father stood on this island, he was a respected scientist who had come to study this small unknown land. But he was tricked. The bacterium was already known and he was tricked into breathing in its poisonous OxqA gene. They wanted to use him as a guinea pig, and experiment on him. But the bacteria was stronger than they had anticipated and any attempts to save him were lost. So I came to the island with the intent of punishing them, and turned their robotics against them, creating a new species of human I have created an army from their bodies that one day I will use to maximize my own wealth and power. Your airplane was perfect timing, we are recruiting.'

'We would never join you.' Kyle shouted again and he pulled the gun from his pocket and aimed it at Adam. His hands were shaking, and Adam simply smiled and clicked his fingers. Suddenly the rows of seats around the ring filled with OxqA.

'Young man, you are not going to escape, so I suggest you lower your weapon before you get hurt.'

Kyle and his dad watched as they became surrounded, all seemed lost.

'We will never surrender to you.' Kyle said, the gun still pointed at Adam.

'Maybe not, however this may change your mind.' He again clicked his fingers, and the door behind them opened. Kyle and his dad turned, and their jaws dropped at what walked in. It was Kyles mother, but not as they knew her. She had been turned into one of them. Half human, half robot.

'Please let me introduce you to one of the newest recruits to our organization.' Adam laughed.

No!' Kyle screamed. He raced to his mums side looked her dead in the eye, she barely moved and her eyes continued to stare forward. 'Mum?' Kyle said as he took her hand. Her head turned to look at him and her mouth began to open.

'Kyle?' She sounded exactly the same.

'Kyle…Kyle?'

'Kyle, wake up Kyle, we are about to land, you need to put your seat back to the upright position.' His mother groaned in his ear.

'What…oh, right, yes.' Kyle sat up in his seat

and looked around. The sun was shining bright through the window and the ground was getting close as they prepared to land.

'Ladies and gentlemen.' The captain's voice sounded over the speaker. 'Welcome to LAX international airport. The local time is 11.20AM on the 24th December. On behalf of myself and the team I would like to thank you for flying with us today and we wish you all a very merry Christmas.'

ACKNOWLEDGEMENTS

I would firstly like to thank Luke Bateman for taking the time to write the story OxqA especially for this book, although I have never met Luke or his family I feel I got to know them all during this process and it has been a pleasure.

Secondly, as always my long suffering husband, who is always a huge source of encouragement during my writing projects and who isn't afraid to tell me if something sucks.

I would also like to thank fellow Author Rose English, who after reading one of these stories over a year ago convinced me that putting together this book was a great idea.

Lastly I would like to thank everybody who has read my books – your reviews on Amazon and Goodreads are very much appreciated, and seeing them all and the love you have shown towards me and my books is overwhelming. For that reason you encourage me to keep writing, and publishing.

Thank You!

ABOUT THE AUTHOR

Chris Turnbull was born in Bradford, West Yorkshire, before moving to Leeds with his family. Growing up with a younger brother, Chris was always surrounded by pets, from dogs, cats, rabbits and birds…the list goes on.

In 2012 Chris married his long term partner, since then he has relocated to the outskirts of York where the couple bought and renovated their first home together.

Chris now enjoys his full time employment at the University of York and spends his free time writing, walking his Jack Russell, Olly, and travelling as much as possible.

For more information about Chris and any future releases you can visit:

www.chris-turnbullauthor.com
facebook.com/christurnbullauthor
Twitter:@ChrisTurnbull20

BEHIND THE MAGIC

Christmas has always been one of my favourite times of year. From the decorations, food and drink, attending Christmas markets and events, and of course meeting up with friends and family.

I originally wrote 'A Christmas Spirit' (a modern day scrooge story) over five years ago. As a lover of Charles Dickens and the original story I wanted to do a more up to date version. The version in this book has had a couple of tweaks from my original, but follows the same story line.

Writing silly Christmas rhymes is something I have done for a long time, most of which were never kept and I regret that now. The ones in this book are either the ones I kept (or remembered enough to re-do) or are brand new.

In the summer of 2016 I wrote 'The Grinch was a Prince' – a strange thing to write in summer I'm sure you will agree. Again I am a huge fan of the original, and especially the cartoon and then Jim Carrey film. After writing it I sent it to a friend to read, and her enjoyment and encouragement is the real reason why I was inspired to put this book together. I wrote new stories, collected together the ones I already had and over the course of 18 months put together a little festive treat, which I hope you enjoyed.

Christmas Game Answers

1. FRUIT CAKE
2. CANDY CANE
3. DECORATE
4. SANTA CLAWS

A HOME FOR EMY

Inspired By True Events.

On a cold October morning a young Border Collie and her litter of puppies are abandoned at an animal shelter. Taken in and cared for - one by one they are found a new home. The smallest of the pups, Emy, waits and watches as her brothers and sisters leave. All she wants is to find a home in time for Christmas.

A beautifully illustrated book about a young dogs wish to find a home.

RECOMMENDED BY CHRIS...

'A grandfather clock has a face and a voice. As its name suggests, it is more than a piece of furniture; it is a member of the family'
Richard C.R. Barder 1983

DECEMBER 1880. There will be no jolly Christmas cheer this year. The harsh winter had descended; snow blankets the ground and the lake is frozen solid. Within the walls of Clement Cottage, the fire is dwindling, its embers barely bright enough to cast the shadow of the broken man upon the wall. Cole is lost in his deep sadness; he has just one heartfelt wish. To be re-united with his beloved, the soulmate so cruelly stolen from him - Cornelia.

A sad mournful ticking comes from a blackened corner of the parlour where a longcase clock is hidden. Tall and stately, noble of face, loud of voice and keeper of great secrets, he is Grandfather Time. Bestowed with the gift of magic from Old Father Time himself, as he begins to chime out the magical hour of midnight, can he grant Cole his wish?

https://roseenglishukauthor.wordpress.com/
facebook.com/RoseEnglish.UK.Author

20103670R00109

Printed in Great Britain
by Amazon